T0277311

My
Armenian
Friend

My Armenian Friend

A Novel

Andreï Makine

TRANSLATED FROM THE FRENCH
BY GEOFFREY STRACHAN

Arcade Publishing • New York

First published in the French language as *L'ami Arménien* by Editions Grasset et Fasquelle, Paris, in 2021.

The Translation first published by Mountain Leopard Press, an imprint of Welbeck Fiction Limited, part of Welbeck Publishing Group Based in London and Sydney.

Arcade Publishing books may be purchased in bulk at special discounts for sales promotion, corporate gifts, fund-raising, or educational purposes. Special editions can also be created to specifications. For details, contact the Special Sales Department, Arcade Publishing, 307 West 36th Street, 11th Floor, New York, NY 10018 or arcade@skyhorsepublishing.com.

Arcade Publishing® is a registered trademark of Skyhorse Publishing, Inc.®, a Delaware corporation.

Visit our website at www.arcadepub.com.

10 9 8 7 6 5 4 3 2 1

Library of Congress Cataloging-in-Publication Data is available on file.

Cover design by Brian Peterson
Front cover photograph by Getty Images

Print ISBN: 9781950994465
Ebook ISBN: 9781950994472

Printed in the United States of America

For Dominique Fernandez

TRANSLATOR'S NOTE

ANDREÏ MAKINE WAS BORN AND BROUGHT UP IN RUSSIA, BUT *My Armenian Friend*, like his other novels, was written in French. The book is set in Russia and the author uses a number of Russian words in the French text which I have retained in this English translation. These include *izba* (a traditional wooden house built of logs), *kolkhoznik* (a worker on a kolkhoz, a collective farm in the former Soviet Union), and *zek* (a prisoner in one of the Soviet corrective labor camps). The Russian version of the adjective "Stakhanovite" was used in Soviet propaganda with reference to workers who were exceptionally productive or zealous.

I am especially indebted to the author for his comments and suggestions and to a number of other people for their advice, assistance, and encouragement in the preparation of this translation. To all of them my thanks are due, notably Willem Hackman, Ali Holloway, Simon Strachan, Susan Strachan, Roger Watts, and Helen Williams.

G.S.

I

"HE TAUGHT ME HOW TO BE SOMEONE I WAS NOT."

When I was young, that was the way I used to refer to how meeting Vardan opened my eyes to the mystery and paradox that underlie the workings of this world.

Nowadays, what I see are no longer obscure enigmas and astounding paradoxes but this simple truth which, thanks to him, I finally came to understand: when we resign ourselves to giving up the search for the other being that we are, it kills us long before we die—in that frenzied and voluble play of shadows which is regarded as the only life possible. Our life.

That evening he was speaking in a calm, slow voice that sounded like an echo, muted by coming from a long way off. His normal voice. Yet what he was saying seemed to be on the verge of madness. Or was he making fun of me? During the early days of our friendship I had sometimes had that feeling.

"Would you like me to touch the sky? Like that, with my fingers?"

I shook my head, with a wary laugh. Vardan raised his hand and remained perfectly still for several seconds, time enough for me to grasp the truth of what he was saying. Seeing that I still failed to understand, he explained, but so unbelievable did the fact seem to him that he was unable to hide his own amazement.

"Just here, as high as we can reach, it's the same air as up among the clouds, is it not? So the sky actually starts here and even lower down. Very close to the ground—under the soles of our shoes, in fact!"

Taken aback by his reasoning, I was on the point of starting to argue about the different layers of the earth's atmosphere, the multiplicity of which we studied in our geography lessons. All those cirrus, nimbus, and altocumulus . . .

Fortunately, I held back from contradicting him and thanks to that brief period of silence between us, those minutes would remain intact in my memory, untainted by the verbal hocus pocus of erudition. A low sun, the serenity of the last days of August, the gilded transparency of the leaves on the trees, a sky that still retained the velvety warmth of late summer—and a boy's hand, its fine fingers hovering in the blue, against the trail of white left by an aircraft. And we two youngsters, holding our breath on the brink of a modest and dizzying revelation.

As I grew older, I would come to understand the true significance of that gesture of his. Vardan was opening my eyes to a great deal more than if he were merely trying to surprise me with an intriguing curiosity relating to the earth's atmosphere.

Without really being able to define it, he was talking about a whole new existence, one in which our thoughts could escape from the rules of this world, one that offered us another way of living and seeing. Our reason, with all its brutal realism, was opposed to this, but within us there was a mysterious will that asked no more than to be able to explore the volatility of this sky that had just opened up beneath our feet.

At all events, discovering how the sky reached down and brushed against the ground and all the cigarette stubs, smears of mud, and spittle that covered it, was for me just as powerful a revelation as the dazzling insights of a Copernicus or a Galileo. More, in fact, for the heights above us, worshipped as eternal, and celebrated in all religions, had thus lost their proud status as a superior world and were mingling with the breath of us mortals. From now on, if I thought of God, I would imagine a presence much closer to us—very different from the lofty arrogance of the deities worshipped and feared by men.

In my memory now, those moments of silent contemplation, on an August evening, would take on the form of a stained-glass window in the air, both fleeting and durable, resistant to the stubborn workings of that forgetfulness we always end up succumbing to.

Long years later I should also appreciate how it was that gesture of Vardan's, his slender youth's arm, that would subliminally help me to understand the vulnerability of the women I came to love. Bodies threatened by age, souls besieged by vulgarity, confidences doomed to remain unspoken in the face of the monolithic certainties of existence.

That hand reaching out and touching the sky would become a secret reason for hope.

ANOTHER REVELATION I OWED TO VARDAN WAS A GOOD deal more disturbing. And yet, in one sense, still comparable to the way the proud vault of heaven had come down to our level so that our hands could touch it . . .

A drunken woman was making her way across some railway tracks, a maze of rails, interlocking and branching off before they disappeared into the mists of a dismal, windy day. Helpless with alcohol, she stumbled, swayed like a tightrope walker, trying to cling to her dignity as she wobbled grotesquely and finally, as if in the end she had given up caring, collapsed onto a sleeper smeared with tar, hunched up and bent in two, like a great bird contorted by pain.

Two men, who were just ahead of us, walking over a level crossing, stared at her and let out a burst of derisive laughter. One of them shouted: "Oi!, Anna Karenina, you want to watch yourself! The Moscow-Irkutsk express is due any minute now!"

Then the other one yelled out with mocking disdain: "No, it ain't, not for another three hours. She's got loads of time to sober up and shift her arse . . ."

As they moved on, several obscene remarks rang out, interspersed with shouts of laughter and whistling noises from the two of them as they imitated the sound of a train coming into the station. A more veiled element now slipped into their mockery. In this I sensed not only contempt, but also the expression of pent-up desire, torn between the attraction of this woman's body and the hazards they alluded to in covert language, whose hidden sense I was unable to grasp. At the end of it all their final tirade, even more agitated and strangely full of rage, made reference to the woman's mouth— her lips heavily made-up with red that spilled outrageously beyond their outline, like a thick coating of paint or blood.

The filthy coarseness of the men's words kept me from understanding exactly what it was they were hinting at. I simply sensed that there was a connection between that half open mouth and their urgent but painful desire.

I was thirteen at the time. Vardan, although he was not as tall as me, was a year older. We cannot, I suppose, have been particularly ignorant on the subject of relations between the sexes. All the more because, living in an orphanage, I was growing up alongside young males and girls, some of them older than myself, who were beginning to embark on physical relationships—in secret, naturally, but without too much adolescent angst. They would talk about all this in boastful, smutty, and often stupidly exaggerated terms, which gave rise to wild imaginings in pupils of my age.

And yet for me the universe of love still retained an aura of archaic purity, made up of inexpressible visions and a vibrant mass of sentimental passions and reveries—revolving, above all else, around the longed-for epiphany of the first kiss.

What struck me that day, there on the soaking wet timbers of the level crossing, was the way in which love—as well as that chaste anticipation of the "first kiss"—was being instantly reduced by the two men to a crude activity, a physical function, the ugly and coarse mechanism of which was painful to me. They seemed to consider that such ways of taking pleasure were legitimate and, when all's said and done, routine, despite some disagreeable aspects, given the filth and likely diseases to which, according to them, anyone exposed himself by consorting with a woman of this type. Then the sudden realization crossed my mind that her coarsely made-up mouth could be used sexually, it could become an orifice with a function, an outlet for male lust.

Within myself I sensed both the death of the person I had been up to that moment and the gestation of another one about to be born: a future man was awakening within me, flexing his muscles and throwing out his chest, and the dreamy child would have to give way to him, deny itself, despise itself for the ridiculous purity of its dreams. And disappear. A sharp pang of remorse took my breath away. I was going to be like one of those two passing men; tall, supremely confident of their own strength and of their right to direct their predatory gaze at women—yes, that woman collapsed beside the railway tracks—the gaze of a conqueror, to whom nothing must be refused. The tempting urge to be reborn with this new male identity convulsed my body with feverish and shameful lust.

The men, still jeering, moved off and we would have walked on after them but Vardan suddenly stopped and looked at the woman intently in a way that seemed to me quite bizarre. We were old enough to know what kind of woman she was. We had more than once seen her pacing up and down between the railway station and a bus stop, then slipping into the station buffet and settling down at a table in the corner facing the bar. Always that heavy make-up, her eyelids charcoal black with mascara, her hair frothy like the head on a glass of beer . . . Now here she was, sitting on a railway sleeper, one hand clutching her chin, as if to soothe a toothache, her legs apart, revealing laddered stockings and lean thighs beneath a lacy skirt that was too colorful, too light for a cold, damp afternoon . . .

We were certainly able to picture what her body offered those men, and, like all adolescents of our age, we could hardly conceal our haste to become such men ourselves. That woman, astray among the railway tracks, was the epitome of all that our ripening virility hungered after. But also of what disgusted us: she sullied our physical longings with her display of worn-out femininity, incapable of inspiring the least thoughts of love. There she was: a great, soiled seagull, a wide-eyed, broken bird. A necklace of pale mauve glass beads, grotesquely askew, had slipped over her bare shoulder.

I had no time to give Vardan a warning or a word of disapproval. He stepped forward, leaned over, and did what I should never have believed possible. With a careful firmness, he supported the woman's elbow, raised it slowly, and after waiting for her to understand his intention, helped her to stand up.

Offering me no explanation, he intended to escort this stranger who was now staggering on her high heels and guide her towards an estate of prefabricated dwellings beyond the railway line, and thence to a doorway, which seemed to be where, in her confused state, she wanted to go.

I followed them and, at the moment when Vardan was helping her to open the door, the woman turned her head and there upon her face, distorted as it was by drunkenness and the stupefying make-up that her profession imposed on her, I saw an amazingly aware look, glinting with tears, a gaze of incredulous tenderness.

No, I should never have had the courage to act as he had done. More than any feelings of shame at approaching this tipsy prostitute, it would have been a reflex of disgust that kept me away from her. A physical refusal to have any contact with such a "total mess": her clothes smeared with filth, her breath sour, her skin which, so the two men had said, must be dirty, dangerous to touch, probably infectious . . . And that mouth of hers, the sexual uses of which they had just been alluding to. Never, up to that moment, would I have considered that such a woman might deserve the least display of kindness and gentleness. Let alone that hand helping her to stand up.

It has only been the experience of close proximity with the bodies of the gravely wounded and the dead, amid the indifferent cruelty of wars, that has enabled me to overcome any such revulsion. Indeed, on a number of occasions I have myself been reduced to a "total mess," a heap of bruised and muddied flesh, one that has aroused grimaces of pity or—more often—aversion.

Yet Vardan had acted without hesitation and with an already adult decisiveness, that of a man who pays no attention to the petty reservations that such a woman might have given rise to. As if he had learned long ago what it is that underlies our physical exteriors that is essential and sublime. As if, in coming amongst us, he had retained within himself the traces of a world infinitely remote from the lives that men lead here on this earth.

A few days later, when we were walking over the same level crossing, this time there was no one about, he spoke in very soft tones—I could barely hear him.

"If they can do that to a woman . . . Taking it for granted that this is all she can expect from life, then why go on with this whole masquerade?"

It was the first time in my life that I had heard such a judgment expressed, extraordinary in its radical force. If one woman's grief, her suffering, was accepted and tolerated by the rest, then this was a condemnation of our entire world!

In our youth we were accustomed to thinking in terms of broad generalizations, dividing humanity into classes, into races, into populations of the poor and the affluent and marking the difference between those societies that were advancing towards a radiant future and the retrograde ones blocking the road that led to this luminous progress. But what Vardan was saying went far beyond this game of social antitheses. The misfortune and degradation of a single individual made the whole human ant-heap unacceptable. Yes, as a whole.

I was stunned by the uncompromising nature of this way of thinking and yet, as I have grown older, a refusal to accept that a single human being may be left to drown in their own distress would come to seem to me to be the only true criterion by which the soundness and sincerity of the finest humanist professions of faith can be judged. A litmus test for every messianic project, for every speech that sings the praises, in purely general terms, of fraternity and sharing.

VARDAN'S STRANGENESS WAS VERY QUICKLY NOTICED—AND caused him to be treated as prey—by those in his new surroundings: the pupils at our school, that other ant-heap, where savage rivalry and scorn for the weak were the rule.

At the end of lessons on the day he arrived they clustered around him in the workshop where we learned carpentry. Not quite going as far as to attack him physically, they taunted him with mockery, insults, and sudden nudges, more scornful than malicious; his small stature and sickly complexion were not worth a real fight. That was how they might have treated a defenseless animal, one not strong enough to fight back but one whose peculiar appearance made them want to shake it, pinch its ears, frighten it . . .

Vardan stood there, unmoving, apparently lost in thought—regarding his tormentors with a dreamy look from his great, dark eyes, not even tucking in his shirt when they tugged at it, squealing with delight at frightening him and relishing feelings of impunity. I could sense what it was that provoked their aggression: the strangeness of his face, the finely chiseled features and his eyes—"Too big," they no doubt thought, as they set about teasing this new pupil. "And with lashes too long, too finely shaped for a boy's. A girl's eyes!"

In the end his failure to react exasperated them. They were jostling him now, trying to make him stumble and fall over, hitting him and ordering him to speak.

"Go on, say something! Tell us something in your fucking lingo! What's the Armenian for 'a stinking little girl's face'? What's up with you? Has the cat got your tongue?"

When one of Vardan's tormentors hawked up some phlegm and spat in his face, I intervened. The urge to sully his fine features, his slim, "feminine" figure, was not hard to discern. I yelled an oath and barged into the aggressor, and now what it was that they had not managed to inflict on this listless youth—a regular beating up—was directed against me, in an explosion of savagery that had thus far been contained.

Fights in the district where our orphanage was located were frequent and furious, I was used to them. The previous year a lad had been killed, horribly assaulted, his throat slashed by a rusty fragment of metal . . . The comment on this made by one of the older boys, his derisive laughter, spat out with fragments of tobacco, amazed me by the element it contained of "practical advice," almost well intentioned. "What a stupid bastard! He should have kept his chin down and he'd have got away with just a scratch . . ." Such indifference to death could certainly be explained by our long and bloody history of revolutions, repressions, and civil strife. And also by the horrors of the last war, which had got the country used to the idea that human life was not worth very much. I can now see that our youth was unfolding against a backdrop of the endurance or imposition of suffering being treated as a matter of course.

That death was the first one I had witnessed and, even more than the mocking tones of that comment, it was the mark left by the fragment of metal on the skin of the boy killed that had impressed me: the rough edges of the rusty metal had imprinted themselves against his throat like an illegible word written in letters of blood . . .

And now, as I undertook Vardan's defense, I probably had an unconscious memory of that bloody "inscription," the "scribble" that had lacerated the very fine skin of the boy's face.

The aggressive fury of those who had been tormenting Vardan was thus transferred to me. Thanks to a swift reflex, I managed to avoid being flung to the ground. I had time to remove my belt. The large buckle on it had been "armed," made heavier by a thick metal plate that was sharpened into a blade at the end. I lashed a zone of survival around me and broke free, mutilating the hands that tried to grasp me, gashing the fists that were flailing in the general melee of the assault . . .

Backing away, I thrust Vardan towards the exit, making it clear to him that our only safety lay in flight. The others ran after us and again I had to swirl my belt in order to keep them at bay and give my companion some leeway to make his escape.

Our flight ended in a district known as the "Devil's Corner," an area avoided by the townspeople, a spot where some weeks previously a number of Armenians had moved in alongside the last remaining inhabitants. These new arrivals had rented a number of rooms there in little houses with walls made of dark brick or cedar logs.

One of the Armenians, a very tall old man—I learned in due course that his name was Sarven—was standing there, at the entrance to this house. The breathless troop of our pursuers slowed down, pulled up short by his intimidating stare and his giant's stature, and began running on the spot. They then turned and headed back towards the town . . . The old man greeted us, myself in Russian and Vardan in that remarkably sonorous language that I soon came to recognize and love.

For the first time I was entering what the other inhabitants of the Corner referred to, using an ironic but affectionate phrase, as the "kingdom of Armenia." And all the evidence was that the king of this ephemeral realm was this tall, placid, moustached man, Sarven.

Having seen off the aggressors without so much as a threatening gesture, he sat down on a bench with his back against the timbers of the wooden house where he had managed to rent a room. The walls had been well warmed by a still mild late summer's day. Above his head a thick slab of plaster had been nailed to the wall. It was pierced by a long iron shaft. This was a sundial he had made—almost the same, he would tell us one day, as the one in his garden in Armenia. The shadow cast by the shaft at the center of a ring of notches marked the hours as they continued to pass, far away in the house where he was born.

As THE DAYS WENT BY THE DETAILS OF THE STORY BEHIND the transmigration of their little community would gradually emerge, with a confidence here, and a guess or a whispered secret there. The Armenians—there were barely ten of them—made no effort to conceal the reason why they preferred this location which people were generally reluctant to choose. They did not want to be too far away from members of their family who were in prison, awaiting trial. From one of the narrow streets in this area on the edge of the town there was a view of a perimeter wall twelve feet high, the dark red roof of the prison, and even the upper layer of windows with bars across them.

But what the Devil's Corner, this half empty district on the outskirts, offered the Armenians, above all, was the chance to move into cheap lodgings, for the most part just a single room, in one of these sad and dilapidated dwellings.

Without going so far as to speak of hospitality, what they encountered there were people who could understand them. The population of the Corner included a good many ex-convicts, adventurers now grown old and weary, wild, root-less people, men whose only biography—as is often the case in Siberia—was simply the geography of their wanderings from place to place. Here in this neglected spot, there was no danger of the little tribe, who had come from the Caucasus and had now ended up beached on the shores of the river Yenisei, provoking the sanctimonious suspicions of respectable citizens or the disdain of those who lived in the town center. Nor were they under pressure to conform with the locals. Indeed, every one of these "locals," whose own lives were a process of perpetual migration, regarded his time spent at the Devil's Corner as no more than a stopover, even though, for some of them, it would last for long years.

As regards the Armenians who were being held in prison, the inhabitants of the Corner showed them a compassion which, though tightlipped, was sincere: what awaited these prisoners was very similar to their own shipwrecked lives.

These shared fates made it easier to admit the truth. In Russia in those days people were extremely wary of exchanging confidences, but little by little the cause of their imprisonment would be divulged.

A few years previously, down there in remote and mysterious Armenia, they had been commemorating the fiftieth anniversary of a vast massacre, a national tragedy, and on this occasion some bold young spirits had taken it into their heads to form a clandestine organization and embark on a struggle to regain the independence of their historic native land. The authorities had not been slow to react, very serious accusations came thundering out: nationalist propaganda, separatist subversion, an anti-Soviet conspiracy . . .

I was in my teens at the time and that is how I perceived the tale of Armenian suffering and hopes—there was nothing in the newspapers about the crushing of the rebellion—but the fact that it led to people being put in prison did not seem surprising to me: our country was forever proclaiming the unshakeable unity of all the ethnic groups that comprised it, and separatist impulses always unleashed a vigorous call to order. And, very logically, a severe punishment. Several Armenians (husbands, sons, brothers), guilty of dissent, had thus been arrested and transferred four thousand miles away from the Caucasus, so as to avoid any inclination towards lenience such as might have been shown by the judiciary in their country of origin.

Having come here to the Devil's Corner in central Siberia, the families of these imprisoned Armenians were hoping for clemency on the part of the judges, trying to assess the likelihood of there being attenuating circumstances. Often taking in a few meager parcels to the visitors' room at the prison, they were counting the days of this "provisional detention," a strange period of time poised on the cusp of a verdict, on the very brink of the camps.

During the weeks that followed I was to learn the history of that discreet Armenian colony a little better.

But on that evening, after the brawl in the carpentry workshop and our flight to the Devil's Corner, Vardan introduced me to an elderly lady who wore a long black dress with a great shawl that covered her shoulders—his mother—with whom he exchanged a few brief words in their sonorous language. The woman looked at me gratefully: I guessed that my friend had just told her about my "heroic fight" with his tormentors. Noticing the scratches their blows had left on my cheekbones, she fetched a little bottle and dabbed them with cotton wool.

It was an ancient perfume, and its powerful hyacinth scent was obscurely evocative of a mysterious happiness that I had never experienced, and this was suddenly becoming more thrilling and intense than all the joys and pleasures of which I was eager to claim my share on earth.

I found it a disturbing sensation—as if someone other than myself had begun to draw breath within me! Yes, someone who had a gift for experiencing nuanced and subtle emotions—quite unlike the reflexes of brutality and endurance a young lad needed for survival on this rough Siberian terrain of ours.

The stinging sensation on my cheek and the lingering aroma caused this moment to last and this calmed the agitation of the fight and our escape. An astonishing feeling of slowing down gave me the time to study everything unhurriedly, with fresh eyes, amazingly detached from myself. I saw this tall, imposing woman, in her mourning clothes, gently smiling at me. I was aware of the intelligence of her dark eyes as she gazed at me fondly, the serenity of her face whose beauty seemed to be heightened by her abundant waves of hair that were turning gray . . .

The sharp scent of the perfume and, still more, the sheen of the intricate silver pattern with which the bottle was inlaid, conjured up the remote Caucasian country of which I knew almost nothing.

Thus, the first impression I had of this "kingdom of Armenia" was ludicrously tenuous: an aromatic fragrance and those colors, black and silver. More than a simple color combination, these shades were evocative to me of a distant past. The objects I had occasion to see in this "kingdom" would always amaze me by their subtle, highly wrought appearance, "too beautiful," I would think, given the simplicity of their function. The constructivist era we were then living through, in which everything must serve a precise purpose and be crudely efficient, made beauty more or less superfluous and favored sober materials, without any aesthetic striving, without the depth of any experience of bygone days. This bottle, "uselessly" inlaid with silver, seemed like an intrusion into the life I had known so far.

Vardan's mother was called Shamiram and, after treating my wounds, she spoke to me in a manner I was not accustomed to and which, simply through the tone of her voice, transformed me into their guest, granting me the status of a respected adult and making unimportant the extreme destitution of my paltry "social status."

"Would you care to drink a coffee with us?"

She spoke to me so formally that I almost looked round to see whom else she might be addressing. A phrase heard in a historical film came into my mind but evidently remained mute there, something like: "I should be honored and delighted!" Alas, unskilled in such refinements of etiquette, I mumbled a dull and embarrassed thanks, blushing and looking down, but Shamiram was already making her way into the little adjoining space that had been arranged to serve as a kitchen.

Indeed, everything had been rearranged in this portion of a house she was renting jointly with two other "subjects of the kingdom." Several shawls, such as the one she was wearing, served as hangings, to adorn the peeling walls, or else to cover the few pieces of furniture the Armenians had at their disposal—among them a couch made up from two big suitcases, Vardan's bed . . .

Years later, when my own youth was becoming increasingly nomadic, I would recall the precarious quarters occupied by this ephemeral Caucasian colony—their humble habitation, which, thanks to the way it was adorned, looked so utterly different from the dwellings in which their neighbors lived. Its "oriental" or, rather, "theatrical" charm enabled these transient residents to create an illusion of comfort and almost of opulence, by means of a few pieces of fabric and strategically placed objects, like the props on a stage set. It was an art common to peoples accustomed to banishments and forced departures, repeatedly obliged to recreate anew their living space—carrying their native land with them in their meager luggage. Yes, to tread the boards of an uncertain existence, to set up the decor wherever the drama of their exile is played out. Those shawls, a pile of books, a candlestick, black with soot, and draped over the low, narrow window, in the place of curtains, those offcuts of purplish muslin, probably left over from some dressmaking project interrupted by another departure.

And even the wind that sent ripples through their almost transparent fabric, this light breeze of the end of summer, seemed to me different, as if it had been warmed by the sun of distant Armenia . . .

Shamiram reappeared, with a tray in her hand: there were three little cups and what I took to be an elegant silver vase. In fact it was a coffee pot. On it, already with a surge of emotion, I recognized the finish—that gleam of silver and black, the color combination which, wrongly, perhaps, I now associated with the "kingdom of Armenia": Shamiram's ash-colored hair, the design on her scent bottle, the dull, shot silk effect of the shawls, and this container, delicately engraved with arabesque designs—"too beautiful"—from which issued the aroma of roasted coffee beans.

No, there was nothing affected or strained about the half hour I was to spend with them, and I ended up almost feeling at ease, despite what had at first promised to be quite a formal ceremony. And also, despite the overwhelming and intense taste, one wholly unfamiliar to me, since the only kind of coffee I had known at the orphanage canteen was a beige, milky, somewhat sickly liquid derived from chicory.

From that first conversation, disorientated as I was, I was left with a single image, luminous and static but dazzling in its visual power. At that time of year (that is to say, the early days of September) Shamiram told me, the transparency of the air is such that the silhouette of Mount Ararat, the mountain that stands guard over the Armenians, can be seen with vivid clarity . . .

Listening to her, I became physically aware of the heady breeze that came from its wooded slopes, the intoxicating air and that sky which, as Vardan had claimed, began very close to the ground—beneath the soles of those wanderers' shoes.

I WAS STILL GIDDY WITH THE IMAGINED SPLENDOR OF THE mountain peaks and the glaciers when the door opened from the adjoining room. A young woman came in and her appearance gave me the feeling that I was still in a dream.

It occurred to me that this svelte, dark-haired stranger might be Vardan's older sister, such was the extreme finesse of the features which they had in common. Dressed in black, like Shamiram, she looked like one of those "daughters of the Caucasus," heroines in the writings of Lermontov or the young Tolstoy, those princesses of the mountains whose slender, gazelle-like silhouettes featured in the illustrations to our books at school and whose immense eyes smoldered with the embers of passion . . .

Her gaze lit upon me but without that wild romantic fire— just a simple note of anxiety. Shamiram hastened to explain my presence. Then, gently laying her hand upon the young woman's waist she introduced me.

"This is our Gulizar . . . When she was little, she had a view from her window of the mountain I've been telling you about."

She made two or three further observations, but I was in no state to hear her: just the name Gulizar surpassed all the aspects of beauty I had hitherto encountered. In her dark head of hair, a very fine, entirely white strand, like a streak of hoar frost, seemed to bear witness to a past and a suffering of which, at this stage, I could guess nothing.

The young woman was holding a parcel wrapped in newspaper tied up with coarse string. The humdrum nature of this burden served only to reinforce the certainty that Gulizar belonged to a quite different world—a universe very remote from this Devil's Corner and the wild expanses of our Siberia.

"Do you think they'll let you see him today?" Shamiram asked her in Russian.

Gulizar hesitated, then replied in Armenian, shaking the parcel a little. Without speaking a word of that language, I thought I could understand the situation: if a meeting with the person she was going to see proved impossible she would have to leave the package—trusting that they would have the honesty to give it to the one it was intended for.

I still remember how, in speaking those last words, her lips took on an expression of rebelliousness, controlled but unrelenting. And in her eyes—that wild fire, so beloved of our romantic authors.

And how right they were, those poets! Gulizar was one of those veritable "daughters of the Caucasus" their verses sing of, a fearless and fiery nature. I would have confirmation of this one day in a street leading to the station from the town center. Gulizar was walking along it, pensive and alone, in a way that set her apart from the other passersby, apparently absorbed by a thought that created a little vertical wrinkle between her eyebrows. I passed her by, just a few steps away, not daring to greet her, let alone to engage her in conversation.

Her sober but elegant dress, her gait, her beauty, and her long silvery earrings caught the sharp eyes of a group of men who stood drinking their beer in front of a booth.

"Hi there, you Caucasian baggage!" one of them called out. "Come and have a drink! Don't be afraid! If you're nice to me, I'll give you a hot kiss! How about it?"

They all laughed, expecting her to react with pious horror and beat a hasty retreat. But, far from being alarmed, Gulizar slowed down, stared calmly at the man who had accosted her and replied: "No, I don't want you to give me a kiss. That cap of yours is much too big."

Taken aback, the man reached up to feel the peak of his headgear and blurted out in a confused way: "Wh-what do you mean . . . too big?"

"Oh yes. It's much too big for the coconut you've put inside it."

And she went on her way, followed by approving guffaws from the company and shrieks of rage from the "coconut."

The expression on her face at once became utterly distant from what had just transpired—as she concentrated once more on that single thought, secret and persistent, one that made her remote from the beer drinkers, as well as from this street, and this life.

II

THE FRIENDSHIP THAT HAD ARISEN BETWEEN MYSELF AND Vardan could easily have faded away: we were not in the same class for our studies and after lessons I went back to the orphanage while he returned to his "kingdom of Armenia" and the room his mother was renting in the Devil's Corner.

My role as his "bodyguard" became increasingly unnecessary—the little bully boys at the school had finally lost interest in their victim; he was too apathetic and paid no heed to their provocation. They were even somewhat disconcerted by the fixed, impassive stare of his great, deep eyes that reflected a universe in which they did not exist, where the respect their combative aggressiveness won for them, in competition with other young males, counted for nothing.

His distant manner was equally discouraging to those who might have liked to become good friends with him and who sometimes, disturbed by his detachment, would grab him by the wrists, shake them, and call out: "Hey! What's the matter with you, Vardan? Wake up!"

And then they would walk away, realizing that, if he had "woken up" to a life like theirs, he would no longer have been himself.

Failing to understand the reason for his loner's distant manner, I was indeed myself beginning to weary of it—rather as, when you have been trying to remember a name, you stop racking your brains and tell yourself that either it will come back to you soon or else that the name is not really important.

I really had no links with the district where the Armenians had chosen to put down roots, this Devil's Corner of ill repute. The encounter I had had there, as an amazed and confused guest, those moments when I had felt myself to be different and dizzyingly elsewhere, all of that was becoming too emotionally vibrant and the affectionate warmth of it too intoxicating, compared with the world I lived in, where one must at all costs avoid showing affection.

I had a pusillanimous but prudent intuition that I should not make another attempt to experience the dazzlement of that half hour, but rather preserve it intact in an aura of enchantment, like the luminous vision of Mount Ararat, like the fleeting—and almost unreal—appearance of Gulizar.

No doubt certain discreet clues, picked up unconsciously during my brief visit, had already alerted me to the fact that behind the great joy I had experienced in the "kingdom of Armenia" there might also lie hidden a great sadness and that it would be better not to add the weight of this to my own life, heavily burdened as it already was, with privation and hardship.

This intuition of mine was confirmed barely a few days later. Passing Vardan on the steps outside the school, I suddenly noticed that he was choking, first gulping air with feverish urgency, then beginning to gasp for breath with a hissing sound . . . He was pressing his hand against his stomach. Thinking he felt nauseous and wanted to vomit, I led him over to beside a tree. Then his pale complexion became blotchy. Patches of red appeared on his changing face. He was turning blue and it seemed to make his skin transparent . . .

Our mathematics teacher, Ronin (a veteran who had lost an arm in the war), was just leaving the school at that moment and he helped me to take Vardan to the sick bay. The doctor arrived a few minutes later.

I waited in the corridor, and as the two men were walking away from that little room the doctor was speaking to our teacher about Vardan's illness in relatively calm and even reassuring tones.

"No need for panic. He'll recover soon. A week, at most, and he'll be as right as rain. And he can go home now if someone goes with him. No, as I was saying, his condition is a not unusual one. At least not amongst people from that part of the world. Given where he's from and these symptoms, it's certain to be the Armenian disease . . ."

His diagnosis struck me as singularly eccentric, to my ears it sounded like a joke and a somewhat crude one! So, a young Armenian could only be suffering from an *Armenian* disease . . . Why not a Muscovite stricken with scarlet fever, or a Berliner going down with German measles?

Later, when I was talking with Shamiram, Vardan's mother, I would learn that this name, without being strictly scientific, was widely used. It provided the uninformed with a terminology that was not too technical and, by means of an ethnic shortcut, indicated one of the peoples—yes, the Armenians—who were prone to this hereditary disease.

Our teacher Ronin asked me to take the sick boy home. In entrusting me with a responsibility which only an adult should properly have undertaken, as if ritually dubbing me, he clapped me on the shoulder—with his one good hand.

THUS MY FRIENDSHIP WITH VARDAN TOOK A NEW TURN—his life was under threat and I was now standing guard over it. I had little experience of relationships between close family members, but, thanks to the Armenians, I was discovering what a family could be, a very special family, it is true, but, for this very reason, one more closely knit, as well as more open to receiving regular visits from a young boy like me, with no ties of his own and, importantly, no need for "parental consent."

I discovered a more down-to-earth advantage, too, in my mission vis-à-vis this delicate youth—the chance to skip lessons in his company on the pretext of illness. This freedom filched from school routine caused us to embark on a new way of spending time together, one in which we did not have to "wake up" to the lives of other people.

Most of the time Vardan had no need to lie about the state of his health. After a period of respite, his "Armenian" illness was returning. It obstructed his lungs or afflicted his joints, causing him to be slow and walk with a limp, or, still more often, it threw those patches of red across his face and body which unfailingly attracted the disgust and mockery of our fellow pupils.

"He looks horrible, that Caucasian toad. Eeugh!" they would say, changing places so as not to have to sit at the same table with him. "Where did you catch it, your Armenian plague? No, keep away! Keep your filthy germs to yourself!"

Without actually knowing anything about it, but with the cunning of those who seek to wound, they had discovered the commonly used name for it, yes, the so-called "Armenian" disease . . .

So on the day of that attack of his which I had witnessed on the steps outside the school, I had walked home with him and told his mother what had happened. Vardan was gasping for breath and unable to speak. Shamiram took a box filled with sachets from a little traveling bag and prepared an infusion, which he drank with silent resignation, no doubt being familiar with medical rituals of this kind. Then he lay down and fell asleep almost at once. Shamiram left me alone with him, telling me she needed to go to the pharmacy . . .

It was a totally new experience for me to thus find myself watching over someone very special, a person who was becoming painfully dear to me as he lay there asleep and defenseless, weak, ill, and vulnerable.

With an ear cocked attentively to the rhythm of his breathing, I stood up and, with a vague feeling of breaking a taboo, I made a tour of the room, this humble fragment of the "kingdom of Armenia" where my friend lay sleeping. Nothing had moved since my last visit: that lamp with a torn shade on the table, the old candlestick, books, a newspaper printed in an alphabet with curiously shaped letters. At the window—the muslin of the curtains . . .

And there, beside Shamiram's bed, those two old photographs, their color turned slightly brown, with the photographer's name in the corner, printed in Russian and decorated with pretty floral motifs. Two family portraits.

I went up to them to study the faces more closely.

I was overcome by an incredibly physical sensation of being plunged back into a very remote era. I became lost in the moments when those two groups—each in their respective photographs—were adopting their poses. In both of the pictures some eight people had been placed with professional care in a tableau of statuesque solemnity, in accordance with a considered arrangement, from which all levity and the least trace of a smile were excluded. The fathers could be recognized from their central positioning as patriarchs, their portly figures and their three-piece suits, punctuated on the chest by the gleam of a watch chain. These heads of families sat enthroned there, weightily hierarchical, beside their wives, beautiful, buxom women with dark hair, robed in black, trimmed with lace. A young man (a son? a cousin?) remained standing, resting his elbow on a pillar, judiciously truncated to the appropriate height. Young women—slimmer versions of their mothers—were leaning on the backs of the chairs where their younger siblings sat. And the background behind, filled with garlands of roses and vines, rose up towards the silhouette of a gleaming, snow-capped mountain—Mount Ararat, of course.

These portraits gave off a feeling of great stability, the evocation of an era when getting yourself photographed was seen as an important and rare occurrence—the crowning of a notable stage in one's biography, professional success patiently built up over the years, the summation of a life worthy of being preserved in the memory of one's descendants. All the members of these two families displayed complete assurance in their situation, with clear evidence of a substantially prosperous social standing, to judge by their clothes and their "bourgeois" appearance, or so I told myself, not knowing how better to define this combination of solemn postures, sartorial elegance, and complete confidence in the future . . . The photographer's name, underlined by a spray of long acanthus leaves, appeared there above the date: 1913.

As I looked again at these people who were studying me, I swiftly calculated the amount of time that separated me from them: almost sixty years! So, the parents were very probably long since dead, but the children had a reasonable chance of still being alive and must now look like Sarven and Shamiram. Yes, he must be an old man these days, that well-behaved little boy sitting on a tiny narrow chair. Dressed in grown-up clothes, he had a very serious expression and was holding the reins of a wooden horse. The same must be true of that little girl sitting stock still on her mother's knee and clutching her toy—a doll with its hands curiously joined together, as if in a prayer, both fervent and determined . . .

"She took it with her into the desert, that doll . . . It was because of the doll they could identify her . . . Otherwise . . ."

Hearing these words, whispered by Vardan, I turned round. He had just woken up. Almost at once, overcome by his illness, he was gasping for breath, able only to expel a string of hissed words.

"As for the others, they couldn't even . . . they couldn't . . ."

I heard the door open and I saw his mother coming into the room. She glanced at Vardan, propped up on one elbow, his face contorted with spasms as he tried to speak to me. Shamiram must have thought he was responding to questions of mine, she could see me standing motionless there beside the two photographs.

"He needs to be left to rest now," she said to me in an unusually cold tone of voice. "He's too tired. You can come back when he feels better. Alright?"

As I came away from the Devil's Corner, I was as intrigued by my friend's interrupted observation as I was sad and vexed at having seen Shamiram lose her temper. She had doubtless thought I was a chatterbox whose inquisitiveness had caused Vardan to suffer a fresh choking fit. And I was very surprised the next day at the end of lessons to catch sight of Shamiram's figure outside the school entrance. Never before had anyone come looking for me after school like this. She addressed me in gentler tones and, as on that first occasion, the words she spoke gave me a feeling of being a very different person from the one everyone else saw in me.

"I was rather short with you yesterday evening. I'm so sorry. Vardan explained everything to me. He's feeling better today. Come and have a cup of coffee with us. That will do him a lot of good . . ."

IT WAS ON THAT EVENING THAT SHE REALLY BEGAN TO TALK to me about her country. Vardan added little, he was still too exhausted, but his remarks, uttered between choking fits, contributed an emotional authenticity to Shamiram's narrative, expressed in the few precious words he would have at his disposal before another attack.

The main effect of what I heard was like a dazzling enlargement, a rapid expansion of the world I thought I knew. A little southern territory tucked away somewhere in the mountainous folds of the Caucasus and scarcely visible on our geographical maps—this modest "Soviet Socialist Republic of Armenia"—suddenly burst forth from its borders and, at the height of its glory, occupied a vast area, one that reached as far as the Mediterranean coast, stretched to the Black Sea, and bordered on the Caspian Sea. This huge kingdom dominated the Caucasus and the lands beyond, extended into Syria and Palestine and included what would one day become the Ottoman Empire . . .

This swift enlargement of a country which in our day was humbly squeezed in between Georgia and Azerbaijan, was all the more astonishing when Shamiram began to run through the history of the Armenian people. In those days, what we were used to was a very simple chronology divided into two by the October Revolution: before 1917 mankind stagnated, first of all in the horrors of slavery, then in the darkness of the Middle Ages, and finally in the hell of capitalist exploitation. After 1917 history embarked on a triumphant march towards the radiant future of Communism.

In Shamiram's narrative, however, the carving up of history in this way became not only artificial but ludicrously inadequate, like trying to measure the earth's circumference with a tape measure. Dumbfounded, I was unable to hold onto the whole sequence of kingdoms which came into being on this ancient land of Armenia, glittered and then collapsed beneath overwhelming onslaughts by invaders. Enigmatic names became mixed up in my head: the kings Sarduri II, Antiochus III, Artaxias, Tigranes the Great . . . And the history Shamiram was telling me, this narrative, as it traveled back in time, extended further still into yet more remote centuries, conjuring up the appearance of the mysterious Urartu, where some people placed the birth of the Armenian nation and its capital, Erevan, a city more ancient than Rome itself! But according to Vardan's mother, their people had also existed before the kingdom of Urartu, for to give a date to the origins of Armenia, it was necessary to go back to ages that no historian had truly been able to explore . . .

A moment came when this account moved into the realm of mythology and took us close to the time of Noah's ark! Had not several entirely serious archaeological expeditions found traces of that bark vessel in a little valley close to the foot of Mount Ararat?

Intoxicated as I was by the way it was all slipping towards myth and legend, I was nevertheless acquiring information of a less fabulously epic nature. Shamiram told me about the Armenian alphabet, created in the early centuries of our era, and how the Christian church was established in these Caucasian lands at a time when so many peoples in Europe were still lost in the sleep of paganism: those primitive Europeans, she explained, "used to cut the throats of animals in the belief that the poor creatures' sufferings were pleasing to their bloodthirsty gods."

But Shamiram's tone was not tainted by any nationalistic bragging, although her words made me aware of her desire to convince me and to correct those mistaken views which, according to her, distorted the perception of the history of her country. And the tale she had to tell (I finally realized) was addressed equally to me and to the bedridden adolescent, exhausted by surges of breathlessness, Vardan, whom I had just now discovered to be much more vulnerable than I had at first realized. Shamiram must doubtless be thinking that by listening to her praise for a combative and resistant people, her son could draw new energy for his own daily struggle.

Part and parcel of this fondly patriotic oration was the desire to make me appreciate that Armenia amounted to a good deal more than this sad image of a humble community of travelers, the diminutive cohort of men and women who had chosen our Devil's Corner as their home, four thousand miles from their native land. In just such a way a princess who had lost everything might have spoken, from the depths of her exile, of the victories of days gone by, the names of dynastic residences and the extent of lost territories.

It is, in fact, only in my memory, that this chronicle evolved in a single sweep into one great epic. The truth is that on each of my visits Shamiram would recount one or two episodes, mention several names, a few dates and, in answering my increasingly well-informed questions, would also be giving answers to Vardan, who was now able to speak again, no longer suffering from choking fits. Then all of a sudden, she would break off, her gaze lost in her own memories, her words stopped in their tracks by some secret or some revelation, the pain of which I had not yet guessed at.

Thus, after several days, I began to be aware of a fragment left blank within the fresco that her narrative was gradually adding up to, a zone of distress and silence which she had to skirt round, as she made her way back into a past of kingdoms and thrones.

Conscious of my good fortune, I was a captive and attentive listener, and this enabled me to note a mysterious regular occurrence: often when Shamiram suspended her narrative, her eyes would settle upon the photographs that hung on the wall. It seemed as if it was there, in the days when those two Armenian families were alive, that the frontier arose to a past that could not be told. I noticed, too, that on those occasions Vardan seemed both resigned and withdrawn into himself, and then, from time to time, full of energy, ready to leap into action . . .

From this I came to believe that the true strangeness of this boy was not linked to his nationality, nor even to his failing health, but to that unspoken gap in Shamiram's story—that virgin patch in the fresco, a space stricken with mutism, the secret of which no one must discover, but which held the key to their lives.

I WAS MORE THAN ONCE TEMPTED TO PUT A DIRECT QUESTION to Vardan, to ask him to finish the story his mother's arrival had one day interrupted: the little girl in one of the photographs, her doll with its hands joined together in a prayer that was so bizarrely realistic, a melancholy and touching presence . . .

More than the fear of hurting him, what held me back was my certainty that I should miss what was essential. Asking for, and therefore more or less extorting, a confession could only result in a flat, insincere response or even a half truth.

Noting singular signs in his behavior and his way of perceiving the world to which he seemed to be such a stranger, I preferred to wait. In this way I had the impression that I was gradually gaining a better understanding of the mystery of the "kingdom of Armenia" which had briefly adopted me. And, without bombarding this taciturn friend of mine with questions, I was becoming aware that not everything about him that seemed to me unusual was necessarily just linked to the customs of his Caucasian homeland.

I recall a surprising remark Vardan made one day when the other boys had driven him away from the sports field behind the school. They were forming two teams for a game of football. Seeing that they were short of players, I asked if the two of us could join them. It was not just a refusal but with an almost animal rejection that they opposed to Vardan taking part.

"You, alright," they said to me. "But him. No way! He'll infect us with his bug. He's not normal, you know!"

In Russian "not normal" could be understood to mean "mad," "mentally deficient," or "deviant" . . . The society we lived in, with its messianic project for the new man, ruled out the idea of anything that risked challenging the perfection of this future hero destined for the happiness of the earthly paradise. He must be in perfect physical health, free of all intellectual ambiguity, unencumbered by the psychological flaws that consumed men in past ages. Yes, a fine, muscular creature, radiant and with no doubts. A walking ideological symbol.

Vardan did not appear to be hurt at having been rejected, nor shocked by the fact that the others regarded him as "not normal." To spare me a futile argument and perhaps a fight, he led me off onto the path that wound its way through the midst of the old warehouses with broken windows.

I was struck by the words he spoke softly as he walked along because their sense took no account of the humiliating aspect of his rejection.

"Let them play! They none of them have the time . . ." he said to me with a vague smile.

This remark seemed so inappropriate that I did not even reply, thinking I must have misheard. They did not have the time . . . But the time for what?

In a few minutes we reached the Devil's Corner. This poor district was bordered at its northern extremity by a defensive earthwork, once the rampart that surrounded a monastery that had long since been emptied of monks and transformed into a prison. That was where those few Armenians, relatives of Shamiram, Sarven, and Gulizar, were incarcerated . . .

The far side of this rampart sloped down to a daunting and high brick wall. According to the rumors circulating in the district, the overcrowded cells of the prison did not contain men serving out their sentences but simply ones held in provisional detention who were either awaiting trial or, else, already judged and found guilty, were waiting to be sent to a camp.

Several rows of barbed wire were there to prevent people climbing up—but it was nevertheless a barrier that could be crossed, for here and there, amid all those strands of rusty wire, ways through had been cut. With a knowledge of the terrain that astonished me, Vardan crept through one of the openings, and held the barbed wire aside so that I could follow him. We scrambled up the earthwork . . .

Lined up along the top there were great cubic structures made of plywood on which the surfaces facing the town bore a series of monumental propaganda paintings—evidently placed there to conceal the prison from the eyes of people walking past, as well as drivers taking the road down below, which ran beside this ancient fortification.

So there were about half a dozen of these cubes, resting on concrete bases, several yards apart, each one easily as tall as a single-story house. They bore slogans in praise of the benefits of socialism and on each panel these exhortations were illustrated with a character from Soviet iconology: a female *kolkhoznik*, laden with sheaves of corn; a metal worker, pouring out a scarlet stream of molten steel; a scientist, surrounded by microscopes and great gleaming glass vessels.

These emblematic figures had come under attack from rain and frost, doggedly determined to tarnish and crack the paint. And furthermore, the slope, being little maintained, was swamped with weeds, tall new growths of nettles, and wild thickets of shrubbery.

Still with a confident sense of direction on this spot, Vardan made for one of the propaganda cubes. This one portrayed a cosmonaut gazing up towards a starry sky, his helmet reflecting the light from a sun outside the galaxy. Despite this pose, reaching for the stars, his legs were plunged, up to mid-thigh, in a very mundane fashion with utterly terrestrial vegetation of brambles and thistles. My friend skirted round the cube, picking his way between the thorny strands, and suddenly disappeared! As I drew closer, I saw that one panel of the plywood had been unfastened—at the spot where the painting showed a landscape of craters and rocks. I tugged at this half open section of the panel and slipped inside . . .

The space within formed a room with no ceiling, the inner walls being fixed to thick vertical supports and strengthened by a grid of broad struts. The sky above us was more intense, brighter; it seemed to have changed color. The noises reaching us from the town were muted, but deeper, as if filtered through an invisible sieve of frequencies and tonalities. And our own presence there—which no one could have suspected—also imposed itself with an unexpected intensity; it had a new and almost intimidating significance.

"Come and look..." Vardan called to me, pressing his forehead against one of the "walls" of our refuge. I discovered that several holes had been made there, slits not much broader than the blade of a pocketknife. I looked out. The dark red prison roof, the narrow windows, with thick, black bars . . . And there, in one of these rectangles of glass, a hand that looked as if it was signaling to us but which, in reality, was pressing against the hinged window of a fanlight.

One could picture a crowded cell, the air stagnant and one of the prisoners trying to open this little window, in the hope of gulping in some mouthfuls of a sky he could see there, trapped between the bars.

When we emerged from our cubic hideaway it was already growing a little dark. I was about to tell Vardan how it had all struck me, but he stopped me from speaking.

"Wait. Listen..."

I cocked an ear and in the calm twilight air I heard a series of plaintive calls that might have been taken for human groans, throaty and resonant—but from the melody of it I was quickly able to identify the calls of a flight of migrating birds.

In autumn it was not uncommon to see such long trails sharply etched against the sky above the town by wild geese.

But here, on this occasion, up there on the high rampart, we were seeing them from much closer at hand—or maybe these great birds had only just flown up from a lake to form their winged design. We could see the delicate outline of their feathers, the color of their feet tucked in beneath them and even, so it seemed to me, the expression in their eyes—that gaze resting on two youths rooted to the spot, our faces upturned, standing there in that rippling sea of wild plants.

"Sh! Wait!" Vardan repeated and very distinctly I could hear not only the brief plaintive cries these geese were exchanging, but also the rhythmic rustling of their wings. This sound, which I had never heard before, came towards us, the rhythmic beating against the air growing ever louder, then it was gone.

For several seconds we remained motionless, following the flight as it grew more distant and melted into the evening sky . . .

Suddenly, beyond the low houses of the Devil's Corner, in the direction of our school, the strident trill of a whistle rang out and the sounds of an argument. This must be the end of the football game from which Vardan had been excluded.

He looked at me with a slight shake of his head and repeated his observation, which now made much more sense to me.

"No, they'll never have the time . . . The time to see such a thing."

In the distance, in the glow of the sunset, we could still make out the moving lines of the flight, the white undulation of their wings.

Having witnessed this beauty for the first time in my life I felt sad that I would not be able to talk about it to the others, those young lads, who were busy squabbling on a patch of trampled earth and who would carry on with their games and their jousting, all of which would take them forward into their adult lives: rivalry, fighting for the best place in the sun, the pursuit of success, defeat, revenge. It seemed to me as if the game that had just finished was a prefigurement of a whole way of life, a war of attrition that would never leave them the time to look up at the flight of birds in the evening light of a late summer's day. I felt painfully lost for words, not yet aware that the urge to share that moment of beauty lay at the heart of the act of creation, the true aspiration of poets, something that for most of the time was not understood.

Before we left, Vardan took one last look at the prison windows, and it was then that, feeling at once happy and troubled, I became aware of the secret bond that now existed between us, which seemed no longer to have any need of words. Yes, we were looking at the narrow window which one of the prisoners had contrived to force open and through which he, too, had been able to observe the slow beating of the wings, that free flight, untrammeled by the turmoil of our lives. His gaze, confined between the bars, had probably followed the flight of the migrating birds as far as the horizon as they slowly made their way towards the south.

III

VARDAN GENERALLY AVOIDED MAKING A SHOW OF HIS strangeness—he knew that, given the illness with which he was afflicted, being cautious in his behavior would attract less nuisance and less bullying. But on occasion he failed to conceal the distinctiveness there was about his body, his origins, and his profoundly aberrant way of looking at things and then found himself in the uncomfortable position of a being who was "not normal."

This happened one day during a geometry lesson which our teacher, Ronin, was giving on a voluntary basis to pupils who had fallen behind and wanted to catch up or who wanted to extend their studies beyond the regular curriculum. Vardan was a part of it, sincerely eager to make progress while I, although I had little aptitude for science and mathematics, went with him to be companionable.

When the weather permitted, our one-armed teacher gave his lessons in the open air, being convinced that geometry called for things to be demonstrated in real space and on a grand scale. An asphalt surface beneath the trees at the edge of the school courtyard became his blackboard.

On this occasion, using an enormous pair of compasses made of wood (that looked more like a land surveyor's cross-staff), Ronin drew a circle, within which his pupils were to mark out other geometric figures—first of all a square, then an octagon and so on, each time doubling the number of sides ...

What piqued my curiosity, more than the scholarly objective of the exercise, was this disabled old soldier's deftness. With his single arm he succeeded in managing the legs of this giant contraption, corrected mistakes in the lines drawn by his pupils and, stepping outside the circle, began to cover the asphalt with whole columns of figures and equations, in which I very quickly lost my way.

In truth the real point of his lesson was to guide us towards an inevitable, almost philosophical, conclusion. By constantly increasing the number of sides of any geometric figure inscribed within the outline of the circle, it was possible to get closer to drawing a curved line but without ever quite achieving this.

The polygons we kept drawing, each with its ever-increasing quantity of angles, would always leave tiny interstices between the flawless curve of the circumference and their countless sides.

"In other words," Ronin explained, "to get there you would have to multiply the number of sides to infinity. But since this is only theoretically possible, the circle will continue to be a horizon that can never be reached. Thus, even if our polygon has a thousand million sides, we will still remain inside this circle..."

And, in fact, there we were, he himself and half a dozen of his pupils, me and Vardan included, all of us surrounded by this broad circle drawn in chalk on the asphalt. Despite the gaps in my grasp of geometry, I was gripped by the idea of this fateful mathematical imprisonment—the very epitome of the futility of all striving in life, for the ideal always eluded us, evaded us, leaving us desperately on the wrong side of a boundary that could not be crossed.

At that moment Vardan's voice rang out, with abrupt and trenchant insistence. "No, we won't! It's perfectly possible to get outside the circle! Look, you have to do what those trees do..."

We looked round. A gust of wind, that great sun-bathed September wind, had just scattered a flurry of maple leaves across where we had been drawing, spilling over the curve of the circle and overlapping with the angles of the polygons. The mosaic of colors—red, ochre, gold—made our white lines on the gray of the asphalt seem insignificant and lacking in real life. In Vardan's words I sensed a truth that was both profound and crazy, impossible to explain, to put into words.

The other pupils tittered derisively, and Ronin frowned, poised to reprimand this joker who had interrupted his demonstration. Which is what everyone thought he would do ... But, leaning on his giant compasses, he thought for a moment and then, in very serious tones, he declared:

"You're not entirely wrong, Vardan. That is, if we're willing to go beyond simple scientific criteria. What you've said may seem absurd, but you're really seeking to abandon the measure we judge by. That's so, isn't it? Yes, you're proposing another principle of existence, a different perspective. An extra dimension . . ."

I have not kept all the terms Ronin used in my memory and it is possible that he may have expressed his thought differently, more hesitantly and with more agitation held in check, the real reasons for which I was unable to grasp at the time. What surprised me most was this brief moment of disarray in such a methodical and rational man. As he took on board the idea proposed by Vardan, he began gesticulating, waving his one good arm about. One of the sleeves of his jacket—an empty sleeve—emerged from the pocket into which he normally tucked it away, so as not to be discommoded by it flapping about. His words became excited and for the first time we saw what had always been hidden from us: the fabric of this loose sleeve, close to his shoulder, the remaining stump of his arm was moving, a jiggling movement it was both comic and sad to behold—it was like the beating of a broken wing on a bird no longer able to take flight . . .

Ronin's musings on an "extra dimension," "another principle of existence" remained somewhat vague and difficult for our young brains to grasp. Yet this prospect of being able to think and judge differently about our lives was not without its consequences. From now on I did not feel better informed, but I felt amazingly alerted to the mysterious possibility of choosing not to follow what everyone took to be the one and only permitted way forward. Yes, the possibility of stepping aside from it—and "getting outside the circle drawn on the asphalt," even if it meant being regarded as "not normal."

JUST SUCH A DEPARTURE FROM THE PERMITTED WAY occurred on the day following our exercises in geometry. I was coming into the Devil's Corner to visit Vardan, who was ill and back in bed again. Just across the street from the house where he lived with his mother I caught sight of old Sarven, quietly installed there beneath his sundial in the warmth of the afternoon. Another man sat there, facing him, with his back to me, and when he swung round in response to my greeting, I was astonished to discover it was Ronin!

Such an encounter between Sarven and our one-armed teacher seemed so highly unlikely from every point of view that at that moment I felt instinctively as if I had reached the limit of what life "permitted," I had stepped over its circumference, the very boundary nobody should cross.

But, in fact Ronin's presence there could be easily explained: earlier in the day, during a mathematics lesson,

Vardan had been taken ill and the teacher, who already knew about his "Armenian disease," had walked back with him to the Devil's Corner. What seemed more surprising was the fact that he had remained there, getting to know all the members of the little colony. He was later to adopt the habit of spending several hours there with them almost every day.

For pupils, a teacher is, by definition, a relatively asexual and physically unreal being—one it is hard to imagine in the bosom of a family or with a wife at his side, being embraced by parents or even surrounded by his children. Ronin's life seemed particularly unpromising for the likelihood of marriage or fatherhood—what wife, or what family could we have pictured for this very thin, bald, disabled man with a stoop who never smiled?

And it was only thanks to the conversations he had with Sarven and other inhabitants of the Corner that we would eventually learn just how deeply lonely he was, this melancholy one-armed man who had made us draw all those polygons within a circle from which there was no escape.

When I arrived at the "kingdom of Armenia" that day, I had found Vardan lying in bed, on the couch made from two suitcases, in the room where the walls were hung about with Shamiram's great dark shawls. Hidden behind a screen of rippling muslin, the window was half open—we could hear what Sarven and Ronin were saying to one another. I could see the two of them—one seated on his bench, the other on a chair in front of the entrance to the little house next door, some three yards away from our own.

An aged, rather rickety table that the old Armenian had placed there would soon attract a number of guests, solitary people who were not normally in the habit of emerging from their drab dwellings.

As the weeks passed we would see them being joined by a man who, like all sailors dismissed from their ships, was nicknamed "Beach." And also, two or three former *zeks*, clearly worn out by life in the camps and by drink, who prided themselves on being able to explain to Sarven a series of dodges current in prison life: unwritten rules which the Armenians under arrest would do well to learn and respect, if they wanted to survive amid the brutality of a camp. For example, as they would very likely be assigned to cutting down fir trees with massive trunks in the northern forests, these prisoners should take care to store up some of the resin: the best adhesive for repairing their dilapidated boots, which the administration would be in no hurry to replace. And better still, this "life blood of the trees" would be an effective treatment for scurvy, which would help the prisoners to avoid returning toothless to their Caucasian homeland, after ten years spent in the depths of the taiga . . .

During the days to come, Sarven's guests would be holding forth about such matters, but on that afternoon it was only Ronin who sat there facing the old man, and it was his somewhat disjointed narrative that we found so striking.

As a political commissar in the army during the war, he had taken part in hundreds of murderous assaults where it was his job, and the fact that he was a card-carrying communist, that obliged him to drag himself up out of the trench ahead of the others, while yelling, "For the Fatherland! For Stalin!" to cover the noise of the explosions, and brandishing a pistol, which was more or less useless amid the torrent of bullets and shells.

"In the end, as I held it up, my arm was torn off by a shell splinter . . . As if to punish me for yelling Stalin's name. But in those days, that's what everyone did . . ."

The real punishment had come later when, three years after the end of the war, this mathematics teacher was accused of spreading the poison of "rootless cosmopolitanism" in the subject matter of his teaching.

"It was totally crazy. Even numbers and equations were becoming politically subversive! No, they didn't have time to send me to a camp, just to transfer me as far as here. Meanwhile, Stalin died. I thought about going back to Moscow, but, when it came to it . . ."

He fell silent for a moment, then lowered his voice and continued his tale of a life dogged by misfortune, speaking more quickly now, evidently seeking not to bore Sarven and, above all, anxious to avoid seeming to be looking for sympathy. Ronin's first wife had not waited for him to return from the war—the notion of living out her youth in the company of a cripple had driven her into another man's bed (this man with two good arms). His second wife had herself suffered badly in the war (Ronin had seen her war wounds as a guarantee of mutual understanding). She had died one winter's night when she was traveling to join him in his exile—this banishment to Siberia that was supposed to cure him of his "mathematical cosmopolitanism." In itself, this life story of his, decimated and fractured as it was, did not really surprise us. During the first decades after the war you could hear similar tales in every family: bereavement, broken marriages, soldiers betrayed, disabled men abandoned, old men with a string of medals dying alone . . . What truly astounded us was Ronin's tone of voice, lackluster and tentative, utterly different from his everyday authoritarian baritone delivery, the vigor of which maintained order even among those of his pupils who were the most unruly and savagely resistant to algebra. We now perceived that when we heard him in class, fiercely declaiming his theorems, what we had always been listening to was echoes of the cries flung out long ago by a young commissar as he emerged from the trench, calling on the soldiers to follow him. "For the Fatherland! For Stalin!"

There was nothing left of that resonance in his droning confessional tale. To our amazement, we were discovering an unsuspected weakness in our teacher, the great vulnerability of a man with no friends and, most of all, despair at no longer being able to repair a life so hacked into pieces, one that was as irremediably limited as the circles he drew on the asphalt.

But perhaps on that September afternoon he was beginning to glimpse an unhoped-for way out. The simple fact of meeting someone who, like Sarven, listened, without interrupting him, punctuating this narrative with a series of little nods of the head, sensitive and sincere; yes, the simple fact of being listened to was already on the way to being a blessed rehabilitation.

When our teacher had finished speaking, the old Armenian sighed and, instead of responding by telling the tale of his own sufferings as a soldier, he made no comment and simply turned back his shirt collar, to reveal eloquent proof that the pain was shared . . .

The following day when I came and greeted them, I would catch sight of the "conclusive evidence" Sarven had uncovered: the weather was warm and, with his shirt open at the neck, it was possible to see the beginnings of a deep scar, a hollowed-out cavity where his smashed left collar bone had been.

I WOULD LATER RECALL THOSE VISITS TO THE "KINGDOM OF Armenia" as representing a substantial period of my life. This always happens when exceptional encounters and new, intense emotions cause time to expand as a result of the truth and power of our feelings.

In reality, that exciting and happy period was quite brief, coinciding with the few sun-drenched weeks of a late summer which, that year, seemed to have forgotten to give way to autumn.

As we reached the Devil's Corner, Vardan and I would be making our way along a narrow lane that was the main thoroughfare through the district, following the tracks of a disused railway line now choked with sand, and from a long way off we would catch sight of Sarven, installed beneath his sundial. Three or four of his new companions would be seated around his table and this had been placed very close to the abandoned railway line—it was just as if these men, passengers with no destination and no luggage, were waiting there for some unknown train, now lost in the misty expanses of their past.

Sarven's visitors were partly attracted by his hospitality, of course. A huge bottle of Armenian wine stood there on the table, an impressive, bulbous flask, wrapped in a case woven from long dried stems. The contents of this grandiose vessel, six or seven liters, at a guess, did not cause serious alcoholic damage. The wine was sweet ("lemonade," the guests would say) and it gave rise to a slow and dreamy intoxication, so different from the fierce and aggressive mindlessness unleashed by vodka. Shamiram would bring out a dish of highly spiced sausages and good bread, as well as those unfamiliar little dark gray rolls—stuffed vine leaves.

Just like our teacher Ronin, what the other guests found in these moments of time, spent there like becalmed vessels beneath their host's sundial, was the chance to confide in one another, to "let their souls thaw out," as one of the former prisoners put it, a man with a scar across his nose, a silent man who alarmed me at first, his heavy gaze seemed to speak of such a lifetime of threat and violence. And yet it was he who told a story so strangely touching that it would remain with me throughout my life.

Serving out his twenty-year sentence in a camp in eastern Siberia, he was cutting down larch and birch with thick trunks, in the very depths of the taiga, equipped, like all his comrades, with a saw and an axe. The felling of one tree brought down a bird's nest in which, amidst a mess of broken eggs, a single one remained intact. He picked it up, took it back to his hut and showed it to his fellow prisoners. A somewhat mad idea took hold of them, that of hatching the egg. Taking it in turns, they carried it in their armpits, so as not to crush it, and at night, also taking it in turns, these "hatchers" would fasten one arm to their own chests, in order to avoid any untoward movement ... Sometime later a little bird emerged from it and was fed first on chewed-up bread, then later on seeds gathered in the forest. One day it started to fly, first of all from one pallet to the next, then across the hut and finally, escaping outside, it flew out over the lines of barbed wire and the sinister overhang of the watchtowers, and vanished into the brilliant blue above the taiga ...

The man with the scarred nose concluded his tale with these words, spoken softly: "I sometimes think that may have been the only real victory in my life."

LITTLE BY LITTLE THE EPHEMERAL "KINGDOM OF ARMENIA" revealed its rhythms and its rituals, the slow passing of its hours marked by the shadow of the shaft on the sundial.

Sometimes there was a pause in those conversations by the light of September afternoons and all eyes would follow one of the Armenians who was setting off to see a loved one in the visitors' room at the prison. The men seated around the table, men who had spent ten or twenty years in the frozen hell of the camps, without any hope of seeing a beloved face again, knew that such encounters occasioned both joy and distress.

Most often it was the slim figure of Gulizar making her way up the street towards the earth rampart, then walking along beside those propaganda cubes, before joining the road that led to the prison entrance. The conversations at Sarven's table would break off, the men nodding silently, lost in thought, their faces grave, their heads bowed.

As for myself, the moment when this young woman dressed in black appeared before vanishing round the corner, that moment, which she made unique, was becoming the very essence of all I could imagine implicit in the phrase "falling in love," or rather of everything that went immeasurably and definitively far beyond those banal words. Admiration, adoration, love at first sight, wonderment, none of those things in their bookish abstraction, had any connection with what I felt. The mere footprint left by one of her shoes in the dust along the abandoned railway track—that fine trade delicately imprinted—transported me into a universe in which each object lived in hope of being given another name.

From now on what was most important in my life was what happened in this new universe, where both the places and the days spent seemed far removed from the world in which I had always lived. Sarven's table on those fine afternoons, the dusty tracks of the old railway, the dim light in Shamiram's "oriental" room . . . And also our hideaway, that cube whose tall sides carved out a square of sky that was all our own more alive and, as it seemed, more responsive to our presence.

I discovered that Vardan had not only made holes in the plywood on the side through which we could observe the prison but also on the town side. So we were able to watch the comings and goings of the occasional passerby on the road that ran around the rampart, though these were few and far between in this out-of-the-way district of the town.

This ring road bore the resounding name of the Boulevard of the Builders of Communism. Cars appeared there occasionally and distracted us for a few seconds from our familiar "targets," a mass of abandoned warehouses, the old, low roofs of the Devil's Corner and even, in the distance, the windows of our school and the trees that grew beside the courtyard.

Seen through these slits, people's actions—meeting, shaking hands, parting—lost an element of their obviousness, revealing an arbitrary, improbable, almost irrational side to them. An elderly teacher emerged from the school, stopped, opened her bag, rummaged in it, went into a bus shelter, and stood motionless, waiting for a long time. A woman lost in the middle of a crowd who did not even seem to have noticed her arrival. What was she looking for in her bag? And how would she spend her time when she went home? Such questions would never have occurred to us if we had passed this woman, who taught us history and geography, in the corridors of the school or in the street. But now, this sudden glimpse of a moment in her life made her close to us, touching, a life with its own secrets, which made us want to know her better, to protect her...

We also saw Ronin walking away from the school building in the middle of a small group of colleagues and we could very clearly sense that he was looking for a pretext to "shake them off," without revealing the reason for avoiding them. He stopped, gripped his briefcase between his knees and thumped the top of his bald head with his one good hand (no doubt accompanying this action with an exclamation: "Dear me, I've forgotten it! I'll have to go back to the school . . ."). And we saw him going back the way he had come, then veering off in the direction of the "kingdom of Armenia..."

One day Gulizar appeared in one of these openings that gave a view of the town. She was following the familiar path that took her to the visitors' room at the prison: the lane that ran through the Devil's Corner, parallel with the old railway tracks, then the "Boulevard" with its worn asphalt surface that led round the rampart topped by the plywood cubes covered in slogans and symbolic figures...

I had the feeling that my life, my breathing, my thoughts, no longer had any other reality. My vision was wholly focused on that trail of footprints in the dust of the path, on the dark lines of the long dress Gulizar was wearing, on the expression on her face, indistinguishable at this distance, yet which I could guess at, thanks to some unknown faculty, superior in finesse and power to all the other senses I had at my command.

Gulizar raised her head slightly, her gaze traveled along the row of monumental cubes, settled on the one in which we were hiding...

For a split second I thought she could see me and had recognized me! This illusion was so poignant that I stepped away from the panel with holes in it and turned to Vardan, in the absurd hope that he might be able to explain to me the giddy, tongue-tied feelings that overcame me when I thought about that young woman. To my astonishment I saw he was leaning forward slightly, with his brow pressed against the rough surface of the panel... His eyes were closed!

Without thinking, I imitated him, closing my eyelids tightly, and discovered in the depths of my vision the precise, indelible image of what I had just seen. A woman walking along a dusty road and suddenly looking up at me. Yes, indelible: so many years have passed and she is still there beneath my closed eyelids, walking along, in the light of days of which no trace any longer exists.

IV

In the course of one of the following days I witnessed a scene which made yet more mysterious the bonds that linked Vardan and Gulizar.

I had always believed that he, a youth of fourteen and she, a young woman in her thirties, without being brother and sister, might nevertheless be growing to be somewhat like this, given the logic of things—the difference in their ages, the uncertain health of the boy, of whom care must be taken, and a communal life which, inevitably, brought the Armenians closer to one another, given the constricted nature of their "kingdom."

That day, on arriving at the Devil's Corner, I chanced on a conversation which shattered that picture of harmony. Vardan was standing on the threshold and directing a fiery harangue into the house, almost savage, to judge from the vehemence of his tone, speaking in the language in which I was already able to identify a few words. Hammering away fiercely, he kept repeating, "It must be done!" like a refrain, and with an energy I could never have imagined, given that his normal manner of speaking was so measured, almost sleepy. But, most striking of all, instead of an introverted boy in poor health, there stood a resolute young man, determined to assert himself, to impose his will, to defy all obstacles.

I could not see Gulizar, but I could hear her voice dissenting, without much conviction, from what Vardan was urging. I was certain I had picked up a couple of the words she repeated several times: *anhnarin*—"impossible," and *Khelagar*—"a madman."

At that moment Vardan caught sight of me, toned down the ardor of his words, and finished off what he was saying in Russian (he had always made a point of not excluding me from conversations between the Armenians).

"A madman? Yes, perhaps . . . Very well, so that's how you see it, Gulizar. But think about it. And whatever you do, don't forget the proverb: 'While the wise man is still thinking about it, the madman crosses the river.' And the river I'm talking about is not all that wide . . ."

This last remark confused me more. Which river did he mean? Was it the Yenisei, whose broad stream divided the town in two, and was Vardan somehow talking about being able to cross it? And why must this "mad" plan be believed in with such passion?

Gulizar came out, greeted me with a faint smile and set off on her habitual path—following the curve of the rampart. Under her arm she was carrying a parcel wrapped in newspaper, a package smaller than on previous occasions.

Vardan invited me to come into the room where he and Shamiram lived. We spent a moment there, not knowing what to do. Myself, silent, intrigued by the scene I had just been an involuntary witness to. He, pacing up and down abruptly yet with a degree of hesitation, still visibly fired up by his argument with Gulizar. He was making gestures of refusal, looking at me without seeing me and finally went and closed the window—the wind, which had become icy for the last few days, had been stirring the curtains and blowing them out through the casement. I noticed that Sarven had not come out to sit at his table and that his guests, too, wary of that luminous but biting blast, had preferred to stay at home.

All at once Vardan managed to master his agitation, he heaved a sigh, expressed in several notes of anguish, and paused in front of the two photographs that hung beside Shamiram's bed. He studied them for a long time, staring at them intensely, as if hallucinating, as if he had never seen them before, or as if one of the people in there might have murmured something briefly to him, smiled at him or given him some sign of secret understanding.

We heard Shamiram's voice from out in the street—she was talking to a neighbor with whom she was going into the town to do her shopping.

My friend said: "Come on. We'll be out of the wind up there with our cosmonaut . . ." and we ran off towards the earth rampart, towards our hideaway, with its panels boasting of the conquest of space amid the nettles and thistles.

HE WAS RIGHT: INSIDE OUR PROPAGANDA CUBE WE COULD scarcely feel the cold of the gusts of wind—and, thanks to the brightness of the sky, it was easy to believe that the extended summer would continue without end. The panel facing the sun still retained its warmth when you touched it.

Without our customary curiosity, we peered out distractedly through the slits in the plywood. Life outside revealed itself in all its tranquil insignificance, only slightly ruffled by the great icy breeze. On the town side the passersby were huddled up, with their coat collars raised, and, on the opposite side, the pigeons landing on the prison roof did not remain there long, taking off again in a flustered flight, scattered by the wind. The watch we kept, I was aware, had lost its exploratory interest—the sense of being immersed in other people's lives was gone.

"Look over there!" Vardan suddenly called out to me in a strangely muted voice. "Look! They're walking straight into the trap, those two lovers!"

I pressed my eye against one of the openings and at first I failed to understand why he was so anxious for that young couple who were walking along the base of the rampart with their arms about each other. Yes, two lovers, probably aged sixteen or seventeen, dazzled by the sun, being propelled from behind by the wind, which must have enhanced the intoxicating illusion they had of gliding along amid the airy luminosity of the day. The girl's russet hair floated up above her like a fine rippling plume, the boy's coat was flapping violently in the wind, in a manner worthy of a scene in a film. No, there was absolutely nothing alarming about this radiant stroll of theirs.

I moved away from the panel, with a puzzled little laugh: maybe Vardan meant that those two would one day marry and end up as aged cantankerous spouses? Was that the trap? In fact, the only surprising thing for me was seeing such a smartly dressed couple (they were certainly young people from well-off families) venturing into our wretched part of town, on this "boulevard" ring road, in the midst of a derelict industrial site.

"Look over to the right, round the corner" he whispered urgently, and I was aware that he was feverishly tense.

I did as he bid me, I looked through a slightly broader slit and I finally saw what had put him on the alert. Along one of the passages that ran between the old warehouse buildings, a group of young men was heading towards the road beside the rampart. These were not the little tribes that made trouble at our school but much older louts, one of the gangs that used to divide up the working-class districts of the town between them.

They were moving along in accordance with a certain hierarchy: the leader, more hefty and dressed more snappily than the others, with his right-hand man beside him, who looked like a huge wild boar, and his two henchmen. These were the shock troops, ready for any mischief there was to be committed. Behind them trotted a number of underlings, novices whose only desire was to win promotion within the ranks. The whole troop had the look of a mob on the rampage, ready to pounce on prey of any kind.

The prey—that couple of young lovers—were drawing close to the corner, on the far side of a vast warehouse with broken windows, and had not, as yet, seen the mob. The likely turn of events was easy to predict: the boy savagely beaten up and held at knife point while they flung his sweetheart down at the foot of one of these brick walls and took it in turn to rape her. Or even, the two lovers repeatedly stabbed, then stripped of their worldly goods and left there, like the carcasses of two herbivorous creatures, incapable of defending themselves. Such incidents appeared in the news from time to time and, amid the routine of daily, almost carefree, violence that we knew during our youth, not many people were surprised.

In barely a minute's time the two groups would meet at the corner of the building . . .

What I heard next made me jump out of my skin. A low moaning sound, of an almost inhuman force, suddenly filled our cube, a mournful bellowing. Called forth from deep within an animal—a big cat, attacking, or dying. I did not recognize Vardan: crouching, his face turned into a mask of horror, his mouth gaping wide; it was he who was uttering these horrible moans.

Breaking off for a moment, he whispered: "Have a look! Where are they, those two?"

And immediately began roaring again.

Guessing what he was up to, I pressed my eye against one of the slits. The couple had stopped and the girl was gesticulating, shaking her head and visibly pointing out to the boy the risk in continuing their walk to the sound of these monstrous moanings. He looked as if he wanted to brave the danger, but a new guest of wind must have carried with it a bellowing sound more fearsome than before. They turned about and started to walk more and more rapidly, retreating along one of the sinuous passageways that wove its way round a former storehouse.

The gang reached the corner several seconds later. The leader slowed his pace, his eyes sweeping the area from left to right, as if he had sensed the proximity of the prey that had just eluded him. His acolytes headed towards the nooks and crannies formed by the walls of the warehouses and one of the little hooligans among the various minions ran over to the foot of the rampart, and pointed up at the cubes, indicating that the noise probably came from up there. With a swift movement of his chin, the leader gave the order and the whole gang, apart from himself and his right-hand man, began scrambling up the slope.

The strands of barbed wire impeded their ascent—we could hear them cursing as they were caught up amid the entanglements. But soon, through our viewing slits, we could see their heads bobbing about amid the thickets . . .

I removed my belt with its armed tip, preparing to lash the first one who appeared in the opening to our hideaway. The chances of our escaping from there were small. The barbed wire would have made our flight impossible, and I was going to be alone in my fight against these youths who were older than me and who would not hesitate over striking to kill.

With a gesture of my thumb, I ordered Vardan to remain behind me, so as to avoid his being knocked over and trampled on when the attack came. It was then that, very calmly, he shook his head and I saw in his hand, pressed against his hip, a very fine stiletto, a sharp, narrow dagger on the hilt of which the "Armenian" colors alternated: brilliant silver and the sheen of black.

Visible now in his face, which generally had a distant, dreamy look, there were elements of hardness and defiance, his great dark eyes, far from showing melancholy indifference, were screwed up, as if better to focus on the target. The devastating realization shot through my mind that this boy, whom it was my mission to protect, was willing to die to protect me . . .

This discovery, so new to me, kept me from keeping an eye on how the gang were approaching and I had a shock when the voice of one of the thugs yelled out close at hand, on the other side of the panel.

"There's nobody up here, boss. And it's full of fucking stinging nettles! They don't half sting! And, what's more, these sodding bushes are full of thorns!"

We waited there, without moving, then pressed our eyes to the plywood. Half a dozen young men were making their way back down the rampart, picking their way through the barbed wire and the wild vegetation. And at the far end of the warehouse area the two lovers were turning off into a street that was more or less civilized—there were a few shops and bus stops on it.

An idea difficult to grasp began taking shape in my mind, a realization that was a source both of enthusiasm and vague despair. Vardan got there first and found the words I was looking for, to express the sense of our melancholy victory.

"We were a bit like the hand of fate for that Romeo and his Juliet, weren't we? If we hadn't bawled out like madmen, they wouldn't be there now, strolling along arm in arm . . . It's strange to think that they'll never know what bellowing god it was that saved them. In fact, the whole course of their lives would have been different if we hadn't made that din!"

I found it flattering that he was generously sharing with me the successful outcome of his ruse. But thoughts of this undeserved honor quickly gave way to the idea I had been struggling to formulate, which suddenly became very clear. The realization that all the time our lives were hurtling along on the brink of the abyss, but that, by one simple action, we could help another human being, hold them back from falling, save them. Almost playfully, we were capable of being a god for our fellow man!

I also sensed that, by making light of it, Vardan had sought to conceal the violent tension he had just lived through, yes, the sensation of having seen the shadow of death pass close by, a feeling with which, on account of his illness, he had long been familiar.

He made no further reference to our narrow escape. On our return to the Devil's Corner, back in Shamiram's room, he stopped in front of the two old family photographs. As he looked at those faces he seemed to be asking them a question and awaiting a reply. In the end he spoke soflty, recovering his normal voice, calm and monotonous, but on this occasion marked by a sadness that was therefore all the more noticeable.

"They had no god to help them. No divinity who might have called out. Nobody. As if the whole universe had fallen silent."

His head was bowed and he spoke with no changes of intonation, not seeking to move me. No gesture stirred his hands which were laid across his chest. His body, motionless, struck no pose.

As he spoke, Vardan looked like a man who is shielding the flickering flame of a candle as he advances through darkness.

HAD HE SPELLED OUT THE CHRONOLOGY OF WHAT HAPPENED, fulminated against the hatred that inflames different peoples against one another, and had he, in talking about the lives of those two families, sought to explain, to offer reasons, had he put a figure to the number of victims, I should doubtless never have experienced that feeling of intense closeness to those people looking back at me, lost, as they were, in the time of those old photographs. I should have listened, taking note of the list of massacres while reflecting, yes, but, after all, this was just one more tragedy in a century drenched in blood.

Many years later I would learn that what happened was that a million and a half people were wiped out. But even this total of lives forfeited, if Vardan had mentioned it in his story, would have got lost, among all the other head counts of extermination: in Russia almost forty million killed in the revolution and under Stalin; millions, known or unknown, annihilated in the Nazi camps . . . Once you start counting in millions all capacity to be moved loses its edge, the most sincere desire to feel sympathy grows weak. And the study of the particular historical situation leads, whether we wish it or no, to analysis, to the examination of the facts, an exposition of the reasons, which veers dangerously close to justification. I remembered how, in the days of my childhood, there were adults who continued to admire Stalin and found ways of explaining the period of the purges. They often ended up by finding this excuse for the horror of all those massacres which purported to be necessary for the future benefits revolutions and civil wars would bring: "When you cut down a forest, chips of wood are bound to fly!" Yes, those human wood shavings, those lives sacrificed beneath the axe of the makers of History.

No such deadly accountancy, with its attendant controversies, muddied Vardan's words, the very simple story he told remained pitilessly transparent from start to finish.

Two families, quite similar in the tranquility and comfortable circumstances of their daily lives, as well as in their unblemished loyalty to the Ottoman Empire, of which they regarded themselves as faithful and respectful subjects. Indeed, such a question never even arose: the lands where these Armenian families lived had belonged to their ancestors from time immemorial, and if anything, it was the presence of the Ottomans that might have been judged to be much more recent and more obviously invasive.

But in their milieu the men spoke little about such things, careful not to "make waves" but rather to excel in their chosen professions. The patriarch in the first photograph was a cloth merchant. The one who appeared in the second was a clockmaker.

The two heads of families appeared almost identical to me in their style of dress, their physical solidity, the look they had of being "well-to-do." I could have confused the two photographs with one another and indeed, to begin with, I could only tell them apart thanks to the presence of the children. The little boy holding the reins of a wooden horse belonged to the merchant's family and the little girl cradling a doll with its hands bizarrely joined together, as if in prayer, to that of the clockmaker.

Vardan's inexpressive voice, as well as his decision not to give me every last detail of that carnage, his refusal, likewise, to solicit my sympathy by means of any sigh or gesture ought logically to have attenuated the effect of what I heard. And yet it was precisely these words of his, lacking in any emphasis, and the extreme simplicity of their literal meaning that gave to the horror suffered by the Armenians a truth it was impossible to stand back from, one both unbearably real and like a nightmare.

. . . One day in autumn the door of the house where the Sarkisian family lived is smashed in with blows from rifle butts. The men are killed on the spot, the tiny children are impaled on bayonets and hurled into the garden, their brothers and sisters—who are hiding amid rolls of fabric—are captured and stabbed. The women are raped on the same pile of fabric, then disemboweled and disfigured. The decapitated head of the father of the family is placed on the living room table—the army photographer takes several pictures, allowing himself, like a true artist, plenty of time to immortalize the heroes as they pose with their trophy, displaying on their chests decorations they have been awarded for previous exploits.

On another day in autumn, or possibly the same one, it is not soldiers from the regular army in this case but a group of auxiliaries, made up of ex-convicts and militiamen hastily pressed into service, that bursts into the house of Alturian, the clockmaker. This man, more combative or, very likely, better forewarned than the merchant, offers energetic, fierce, relentless resistance. He has no weapons to hand but defends himself by taking down heavy clocks from the walls of his workshop and hurling them at the band attacking him. These exploding timepieces clearly make an impression on the aggressors—the battle lasts longer than the similar slaughter in other places. As this man defends his family, he is stunned to notice there, in the thick of this mob of killers, several neighbors of his, who only the day before would greet him respectfully in the street. Once his supply of weapons—clocks under repair—has run out, he lifts up his worktable and hurls the oak mass of it against a spiral staircase which collapses, thus cutting off access to an upper room where his wife and children have taken refuge. He is killed by one thrust of a cutlass in his back. The respite gained, thanks to the collapse of the staircase, allows for his family not to be slaughtered on the spot. These survivors are impressed into a convoy heading towards Syria. A journey of murderous slowness—half the exiles die of thirst, of hunger, of suffocation. Some of them are interned in camps where they are left to die. Others, like that little girl, still clutching her doll, embark on a deadly march across the desert. Mercenary soldiers, recruited among released prisoners, pursue them, rob them, rape them, kill them. It will be possible to identify the clockmaker's daughter thanks to that toy—a doll with its hands joined together, exactly like in the photograph, in an involuntary imitation of prayer . . .

I no longer recall whether my silence at the end of this recital was caused by stunned feelings or rather by my swift realization of how utterly pointless, almost absurd, it might have been for me to make a remark of any kind. At all events, over the course of many long years, I would thank whatever guardian angel it was that caused me to refrain from all reaction, the least judgment or comment.

For a long while I did not stir, feeling no embarrassment at my silence, having suddenly grown up, or been aged, my young life immeasurably prolonged by the whole duration of these shattered life stories I had just made room for in my memory, and whose likenesses were staring out at me, each in their own way, from the faded brown surfaces of the two photographs.

The door opened, Shamiram came in carrying a large shopping bag. Her voice, although she was speaking in Russian, seemed to resonate with a strange time lapse before I could understand her . . . Vardan, too, looked as if he was not hearing her, but guessing at what she was saying from the movement of her lips.

"Right, I'm going to make you a nice cup of coffee . . ." she said, stepping into the alcove that served as a kitchen.

The distance that now lay between me and my earlier life could be measured by this detail: when Shamiram returned she was not carrying her silver coffee pot, but a little aluminum saucepan from which she filled our cups. In the state I was in, I was not even capable of noticing the difference.

It was only a week later that I learned the reason for it: for some time now, in order to provide wherewithal for their "kingdom," the Armenians had begun selling the few objects of value that they possessed.

V

I REALIZED HOW WELL I HAD COME TO KNOW VARDAN NOW on the day when I detected an unfamiliar tone of voice in the way he told me of a plan of his. With a gleeful enthusiasm that was not like him at all and which worried me, he began talking about a "highly confidential" piece of information gleaned from "an old history book." To emphasize the air of mystery, he spoke in a whisper. So, according to this legendary document, there was evidence that at the moment when the monastery was shut down and transformed into a prison, the monks had buried their "relics of gold" in a cache at the top of the rampart. And, by an even more incredible coincidence, the spot where these things had been buried was located beneath the cube that was our hideaway!

I ought to have given him a more cautious, more adult response, or, quite simply, a somewhat teasing one, but, after what he had told me about the two photographs of the

Armenian families, yes, after that abrupt onset of maturity which, in one sense, brought to an end the only life I had known up until then, I was tempted to revert to the carefree mood of adolescence, the age that was mine, the age when you still think you may one day land on a treasure island.

This urge to shed the burden of those griefs of long ago (the Armenian tragedy, a memory I had not really chosen to share) caused me to agree to Vardan's proposal with some-what exaggerated, but, after all, quite natural enthusiasm. It would have been the same if he had suggested going to see an adventure film or a comedy, either of which would have given me a brief interlude of forgetfulness and would have relieved the vision I had of that endless procession of souls and bodies in torment. Perhaps, with this plan to go digging, he, too, was seeking a way of freeing himself from all that suffering in the past.

We began our spadework that same afternoon, following the directions Vardan gave me, consulting a sketch copied from that "old history book" of his. The earth was loose enough beneath the top layer and digging it took little effort. Even without thinking about the treasure that awaited us, I found the task fun. Unseen by anyone walking along the Boulevard of the Builders of Communism, at the foot of the rampart, we were slowly delving down into the bowels of that earthwork, down into the depths of history, as it were. Up above, a futuristic vision was displayed across the propaganda panel: that gallant cosmonaut on his interstellar trajectory. Down below, moving backwards through time, were layers of earth imbued with the grim relics of the Stalin era. Next, descending further, we reached the period when there was a monastery inhabited by austere and choleric monks. And, still further back, it was possible to imagine the long days of back-breaking labor, moving earth, by which this fortification had been raised to protect the town and its inhabitants against the raids from Tatars . . .

A thick, old-fashioned rusty nail with a broad head, a fragment of pottery, or even just a few ancient shards were enough to satisfy our scarcely scientific curiosity. The compressed density of the centuries was becoming something we could touch and even smell, as in the case of some copper buttons, green with verdigris, that had a strong acidic stench when we grubbed them up from between a couple of earthworms and a maze of roots.

Often the real discoveries we made were not what lay embedded in the cavity we had dug, but quite elsewhere. After a day of rain, the bottom of the hole, which now concealed us up to our chins, was filling up with water which we had to bail out with a bucket. Shivering and covered in mud, we now remembered our mathematics teacher, Ronin, and his story: that young commissar who used to leap out of a trench, leading the soldiers into an attack. I had previously always pictured these military hideaways as dry, sandy, almost comfortable places, where fighting men could take their ease between two assaults. Now the reality of war became plain to us: on the contrary, Ronin and his fellow soldiers would have been mired in mud, and, if hit by a bullet, would have collapsed within the narrow confines of that earthy cesspit, brimming with ordure, which would become their grave.

And then there was this other revelation, even more astonishing than that of the filth which had been the infantryman's daily lot. Our well was already deeper than our own height, which made it necessary to use a rudimentary ladder we had constructed. One afternoon, crouching at the bottom of the pit, I looked up and saw a diffuse scattering of tiny lights gleaming in the air, as often happens when, after being bent double over a long task, one straightens up too abruptly. Having paused for a moment, I looked up at the sky more calmly and was astounded to make out several pale, but nevertheless real stars. In broad daylight!

Vardan, who was certainly better versed in astronomy than me, solved the mystery for me: the height of our cube, plus the depth of our well, was making the sky appear darker, which, for lack of light, thus became as it appeared at night—covered in stars. The idea that all through the day the stars were still there watching us, but only obscured by the blue luminosity, and that therefore their constellations never leave the sky, was a discovery a great deal more far-fetched than the lure of some ancient chest overflowing with gold, the unearthing of which, if the truth be told, I had long since ceased to hope for.

IT WAS AS HE WAS CLIMBING BACK OUT OF OUR STARLIT WELL that Vardan felt himself weakening and, gripped by the return of his illness, he had to stay in bed until the start of the following week. I continued digging all alone, working flat out, intending to surprise him with my prodigious output, worthy of one of the Stakhanovite workers of Soviet propaganda.

But my intended performance target was never reached, for on the following day the earth proved more resistant and from beneath the blade of my shovel it threw up a quantity of fragments of bone, both large and small. And suddenly a skull! Then an entire skeleton, oddly lying "face downwards" and covered with shreds of rotten fabric . . .

I broke off from my task and, feeling a twinge of superstitious fear, gathered up the skull into our bucket and then climbed back up the ladder. What should I tell Vardan? At all events, showing him these human remains seemed to me impossible, after his story, the grim account he had given me of the fate of countless families, driven into the desert, who had either starved to death or been shot down, leaving a path strewn with bones, all too similar to those I had just unearthed. Should I fill in the hole again and lie to him, pretending there had been a landslide? Or fill it up with water and blame it on a downpour?

While I was trying to think of some credible diversionary action, a dull rhythmic noise arose on the other side of the panels of the cube and then became louder. A heavy panting sound, not really frightening, but one that nevertheless made me think there must be a large animal roaming about outside our hideaway and snuffling in the bushes.

The plywood panel, already split at the place where we always went in, began to move, gave off the snapping sound of an additional breakage and slowly opened . . . I backed away from it, gripping my shovel, poised to repel an attacker.

And I could not believe my eyes when, stooping because of the low passageway, what should appear before me but the great bald head of Sarven!

At the sight of me, holding my shovel like a bayonet, he gave a friendly laugh and his gaze traveled in a long, circular path to take in the curiosities with which our hideaway was furnished: two old stools rescued from a rubbish dump, a square of stones, within which we had managed to roast several potatoes, a chest where we kept matches and salt. And this excavation of ours. Sarven walked over to it and peered down to the bottom. He commented on its depth by breathing into a whistle that mutated into the start of a tune.

Then the skull lying in the bucket caught his eye. He showed no particular emotion at the sight of the dead man's toothless grimace, sighed, shook his head, then said to me: "So, you'll stop digging now, won't you?"

I stammered out an evasive reply, saying that I did not want Vardan to discover these mortal remains and that the treasure we were looking for was probably elsewhere.

He listened to me absent-mindedly and went and pressed his forehead against the panel that faced to the rear, towards the prison. As he watched through one of the slits, he made no comment, just matching his thoughts with little clearings of his throat. When he turned back to me, he looked reassured, as if, when he had come to our hideaway, he had been apprehensive of discovering a project much further advanced and more dangerous.

"If they catch you, the two of you, what story are you going to tell them to explain this hole?"

I became confused, not daring to admit that we had not even thought of a vaguely plausible alibi.

"Well, you see, we were looking for a treasure . . . Vardan showed me this map . . ."

Sarven rummaged in his pocket and gave me a handful of coins. I was astonished to see that they were ancient pieces of silver, embossed with the two-headed eagle of the tsars.

"Smear this stuff with earth and if things turn out badly you could always say that you'd found this 'treasure' and were trying to unearth some more . . . Look, there. That's a treasure, too!"

Sarven crouched down amid the discarded clods of earth and retrieved a little rectangular board. He wiped it clean of lumps of clay and I saw that its surface had painted outlines on it, from which one could make out a human face.

"It's an icon," Sarven remarked softly. "Just a very small one. They were known as 'ladankas.' Very useful for monks as they journeyed from one monastery to another . . . The bones that you've found are all that remains of those men of faith. They were killed at the start of the thirties, and were given neither a decent grave, nor even a cross . . . They mustn't be disturbed, agreed?"

I asked him if in that case I ought to fill in the hole we had dug. Sarven hesitated, it seemed as if he was regretting that our efforts should have been in vain.

"We'll see . . . There's no hurry. You can talk to Vardan about it when he feels better . . ."

We left the hideaway. Once outside, we were blinded by a low sun, deep red. Before we set off down the hillside covered in brambles and barbed wire, Sarven murmured sadly: "You know, in our country we have a proverb that says: 'Shamed by what it has seen during the day, the sun blushes as it turns in for the night.' It would be as well if men did the same."

I NOW SPENT LONG HOURS EVERY EVENING AT VARDAN'S SIDE. His illness made him lame and feverish. His swollen knees caused him to grimace at each step he took. To distract him, I would give him news of what was happening at the school and in the town, which helped to alleviate the torment for him of being immobile. As it happened, there was torrential rain during those days, which allowed me to conceal the truth from him: when he asked me how my drilling work was progressing, I explained that the hole was full of water and that, to avoid the whole thing collapsing, it was better to wait.

One day, while we were talking, Gulizar came in and walked through the room as if she had not noticed I was there. A little piqued, I called out to her, using several Armenian words that I was pleased to be more or less capable of articulating.

"*Bari ereko! Quour Jan, anund inch a?*"

My excessively cheerful tone of voice and the sense of the sentence ("Good evening! What is your name, young woman?") came at a bad moment. But, out of kindness, Gulizar stopped and made the effort to smile at me. I was stunned to see that she was weeping! What was most astonishing was that nothing in her calm facial expression gave any sign of distress. The tears flowed over her cheekbones and down her cheeks, without affecting the beauty of her face. From what I had witnessed in life and in films, I was accustomed to heart-rending sobs, noisy sniffles, red faces bathed in moisture. This young woman's tears, as she gave me her gentle smile, were not accompanied by the faintest sigh, nor the least cry of distress. Gulizar walked over to the entrance door, paused for a moment, as if making an effort to recall something, then went out. This time she had no parcel under her arm.

In a final glance at her, I noticed that beneath her hair, which was tied up into a chignon, she was no longer wearing her pretty silver earrings, those with their quincunx pattern whose lacy design was reminiscent of threads of hoarfrost.

Vardan must have noticed my perplexed look. Then, in some embarrassment, almost as if he felt vaguely guilty about the situation, he confided the truth: the Armenians of the "kingdom" were currently in the process of selling valuable objects and jewelry, which would enable them to stay a little longer at the Devil's Corner, as they awaited the conclusion of their loved ones' trial.

This necessity seemed to me so appalling, that I almost handed over to him the silver coins—the "treasure in case of need" given me by Sarven. But some good instinct stopped me doing this, otherwise I should also have had to tell Vardan about the old man's visit to our hideaway, the buried bones and, above all, the fact that it was impossible for us to continue digging.

Disconcerted by this admission I had only just held back, I burst out, in exaggeratedly bitter tones: "But it's so sad . . . all those beautiful things that will disappear! You remember Shamiram's coffee pot. Has she sold that, as well?"

Vardan, who was lying in bed, propped himself up on his elbow and gave me a strangely serene look. His voice responded to my despairing observation almost joyfully.

"No, nothing will disappear! You see, you yourself still remember Shamiram's coffee pot and, with it, those hours we spent together. That time is still in your memory and that's what really matters . . ."

As so often, Vardan's reasoning left me in two minds. The idea that a lost object still survived, at the same time as having disappeared, seemed to me to be both very true and hard to accept. The possessive instinct was linked in my head with the very sense of life itself, with my youthful desire to touch, feel, and hold onto everything that was precious to me. And yet, that silver coffee pot: How can I put it? Yes, he was right— sold, taken away, gone forever, it now seemed much more alive to me, no longer merely a gleaming, brilliant object, but enriched by the light of the afternoons I had spent in the "kingdom of Armenia." And those earrings Gulizar had been obliged to sell, they were evocative now of those moments when she used to leave the house and set off along the path that ran beside the old railway. They seemed to live forever in moments which were far more precious than the metal of those pretty ornaments.

With a disturbing intuition, I sensed that those words spoken by this sickly youth, as he lay there on his two-suitcase bed, came from a still very distant moment in the future life of an elderly man, whom Vardan would one day become, a moment of experience and wisdom, which, thanks to some unknown miracle, he was able to express now.

Seeing me at a loss in my thoughts, he smiled and adopted a gently teasing tone.

"Look, Mount Ararat, the Armenians' sacred mountain, is in Turkey these days. We've lost it . . . But, in fact, not having it makes it all the more dear to us. That's the real choice: possessing or dreaming. I prefer dreaming."

He let himself fall back onto his pillow and seemed exhausted. On his side table I saw his stiletto, that dagger whose hilt was decorated with the same engraved motifs as Gulizar's earrings.

As I walked away from the "kingdom," I reflected that in a week or two's time that fine blade was going to be sold as well. Possessing or dreaming . . . No, I did not yet feel myself sufficiently detached from this world to accept, as Vardan did, this bitter elegance of loss.

SOME DAYS LATER, IT WAS ALREADY THE START OF OCTOBER, there was a particularly mild afternoon, lit by a veiled sun, and an evening without a breath of wind, the last afterglow of summer. Through the window of the room where I was with Vardan we could hear the preparations for a festive event—a dinner, just a modest one, but one the Armenians had gladly organized to celebrate the birthday of our teacher, Ronin.

They had gathered at the house of a neighbor, Shamiram and Gulizar's landlady. The clatter of knives and forks and the sounds of conversations and toasts rang out in the narrow alleyway, creating the illusion of summer weather, when life spills out onto the warm streets at night. With a hint of Armenian patriotism, Sarven's bass voice could be heard proposing a toast to the health of Marshal Bagramian, "At the start of the war he was one of the first people to succeed in breaking through the German encirclement with his army!"

Other male voices added theirs to his in discordant but passionate agreement.

A somewhat slightly wheezy record player was hissing out songs in vogue from before our childhood, melodies with tunes and old-fashioned words that united the generations of guests. Sometimes the needle got stuck and its quavering repetitions made us smile: "I remember your kisses that evening in spring . . . in spring . . . in spring . . ."

Gulizar was the first to come back into the house, her cheeks a little pink and with an emotional gleam in her eye. Those few hours of happiness and festive solidarity must have given her back some hope.

During the dinner one of the voices—which we had recognized as that of the ex-prisoner with the broken nose—had called out several times in solemn tones:

"Let us drink the health of those who now look at the sky through squared windows! And may they return among us tomorrow!"

For the first time this man was sitting beside a woman who strangely reminded me of another. She had a very plain face, without a trace of make-up, a dull little necklace, her hair gathered up into a modest chignon. Hers was a neutral, silent appearance, amazingly self-effacing. I was nevertheless convinced I had seen her somewhere before . . .

The noise and conversations had ended and I was just about to say good night to Vardan when I saw he had fallen asleep. I left the room on tiptoe and closed the door carefully, preparing to walk down the main alleyway through the Corner.

Suddenly in the darkness behind the angle of the house next door I noticed two shadowy figures seated on Sarven's bench. The light of a cigarette glowed in the darkness. I found I was caught in a trap—I was loath to go back into the room and wake Vardan, but I felt nervous of walking past this couple who were talking very quietly. Particularly as I now shared with Sarven the secret of the monks who had been slaughtered and of our covert digging.

I moved a few paces forward and squeezed up close to the wall, thinking that, as the cigarette had gone out, they would soon be going to bed. And at that moment, thanks to a remark spoken in somewhat louder tones, I perceived my mistake: it was not Sarven at all!

The man smoking was our mathematics teacher, Ronin, and, seated beside him, I now recognized Shamiram . . . I had always seen her as an older woman, almost elderly, and thought of Ronin in the same way, too.

But those were the perceptions of a thirteen-year-old adolescent. That year they must both of them have been scarcely more than fifty.

For me, the questions the man was putting to her somewhat insistently had an enigmatic ring to them.

"So, when it comes down to it, that boy may not be Armenian at all?"

Shamiram replied with a sigh, somewhat embarrassed.

"To tell you the truth, I didn't really ask myself that question when I adopted him . . . The maternity hospital was very close to the village where I was born. Yes, in the Karabagh district . . ."

The way she answered him seemed to me at the time very oblique. This impression was partly due to my ignorance but also due to the heavy lid of censorship under which the very least piece of "ideologically sensitive information" was kept by the authorities. Shamiram would certainly expect Ronin—a teacher and therefore an intellectual—to be well informed about the ins and outs of the situation in the Caucasus, or that he would at least know a little more than was reported in official news bulletins. As a result of this, what she was about to relate consisted of a dotted line of facts, but between the dots there were many elements beyond my comprehension.

Some fifteen years earlier, an ethnic conflict erupts in the remote Armenian enclave of Karabagh, which is surrounded by territory that is part of Azerbaijan. Like a grim replay in miniature of the great massacres of 1915, an abrupt flare-up of brutality runs through several villages with its share of acts of violence. The authorities respond swiftly, the clashes between different communities are put down, the information is suppressed; the image of the Soviet fatherland, united and ardently internationalist, is preserved. A year later all is calm. Shamiram travels there from the capital to pay a visit to her family and the village where she was born. There she learns the news: one of the young women who were raped has died in childbirth, giving birth to a son. Shamiram, widowed two years before, adopts him and calls him Vardan—the name of the husband she had lost (that young officer with a moustache whose photograph I had seen on her side table) . . .

She broke off her story at that moment, remarking with a slight tremor in her voice, by way of explanation of her widowhood, that when her husband had returned from the war, "the trophy he brought with him was seventeen wounds in his legs and head." Perceiving that listening to the tale of a soldier horribly wounded could be painful for the disabled veteran, Ronin, she made haste to finish her story in a few words: little Vardan was to become a young Armenian among others. And, as if fate had sought to reinforce this identity, the child had even inherited that wretched disease they called "Armenian"...

Ronin, absorbed by Shamiram's story, must have tasted charred paper as his cigarette burned right down. He flung it to the ground and stamped on it furiously. In an uncertain voice, in which this fury, resignation over the way fate determines our lives and an unfamiliar, unusually sensitive note were combined, he asked: "But then...Vardan's father—well, the rapist, was an Azerbaijani, a Turk, in fact!"

Shamiram allowed a moment to pass, doubtless wanting to avoid giving a hastily definitive reply and a version of the facts that would have left no room for doubt.

"That man was...his father. Yes, sir, his father. May God be his judge. And in any case, I'm not sure, either, whether his mother was Armenian. Not far from that little town there was a big construction site, men and women from all over the country came to work there. Russians, Ukrainians, and a good many workers from Central Asia. And then, long before the works, there were Greeks there, Georgians, Ossets, and even some Tatars. So who knows what that young woman's origins were? Is that so important, after all? What mattered was that Vardan should have a family. And that he should be loved...Good, I must go and prepare his infusion for him."

They stood up and I saw Shamiram holding out her hand
to Ronin, her right hand, which he took with his left hand,
turning it round the other way as he did so. This clumsy greeting brought them closer together in the shy, timid beginnings
of an embrace.

CURIOUSLY ENOUGH, WHAT I HAD LEARNED ABOUT VARDAN'S origins afforded me real delight, though not for the best of reasons. The feelings of inferiority we all experienced at the orphanage gave us fantasies about the advantages "normal" children could boast of. By now becoming a boy of mixed race with an unknown father and a dead mother, Vardan was drawing closer to us, canceling out our status as pariahs and, albeit unconsciously, I felt a certain gratitude to him for this.

The other aspect of his new identity seemed more difficult to understand. In our country's passports one's nationality had to be strictly and clearly specified; one was quite definitively Russian, Uzbek, Moldavian, or Latvian and so forth, with no imprecision possible. But Vardan? What could he claim to be? In a few years' time, when he received his passport, the question would be posed and I found it hard to see what he would to be able to indicate, as his ethnic origin, on line number five, on the relevant page, where this information would be printed.

The question worried me, but I did not dare to bring it up while Vardan was struggling against his illness, which left him exhausted. I came to see him every afternoon and brought him work from school, so that he should not fall too far behind the others, and, as I looked at him, I never ceased wondering what people he might, in fact, belong to and what was the human truth of this very young man, who occasionally went into contortions as he repressed groans of pain.

An "Armenian disease" . . . So it was that specific physiological and medical condition that was the determining factor! Even though he might not have a single drop of Armenian blood in him? Shamiram's story had carefully not excluded that possibility.

I decided to ask Vardan about it on the day when he was finally able to go for a walk with me into the countryside, among the fields and willow groves that lay beyond the Devil's Corner. For him, climbing up onto the rampart would still have been hard—his aching joints would have hurt him too much.

We moved away from the "kingdom of Armenia," following the road beside the rampart but in the opposite direction—towards the place where an old wooden bridge led across a little river lined with trees. As we walked along, I was preparing my question, by talking about the passports he and I were due to receive in a few years' time and also referring to the variety of origins and ethnicities that swirled around on these Siberian lands—thanks to the presence, whether voluntary or forced, of all the exiles here. But I could see no way of broaching the question without stirring up memories of his whole Armenian past. Besides, did he himself know that Shamiram had adopted him? Had she ever talked to him about that part of their shared history? I was afraid of betraying a secret whose existence might well not be known to him.

When we reached the bridge, we leaned on the parapet to allow Vardan to catch his breath. And it was there, unable to restrain my curiosity any longer, that I asked him, somewhat abruptly: "Tell me, you yourself . . . Do you feel you're more Armenian or . . . just Soviet, like the rest of us? I mean, what people do you think you belong to?"

He remained silent, leaning well out over the river, observing its waters, quite slow moving, as they carried away a multitude of long, gilded leaves. I thought he had not heard me, but I knew I would not repeat the question now, for fear of hurting him.

Suddenly, he gave his reply and his words were mingled with the rustling of the wind in the willow branches and the lapping of the current.

"Me? I don't know . . . I think what I am is just that one there. Not anyone else . . . Look . . ."

Like him, I leaned over the parapet, and in the gray-blue waters of the river I saw the reflection of his face, very familiar yet unrecognizable among the slivers of gold that the wind sent scudding under the bridge, as it stirred the branches of the willows.

"Yes, that's all I am . . ." he repeated, getting this in before the mocking retort I was about to make.

And in that way, he gave me time to realize that he was right. He was this reflection on the moving surface of the river—"in another dimension of existence," as Ronin had put it.

. . . Fifty years later, I can now confirm it, for this face, amid the rippling water and the gilded leaves, has remained vividly clear to me, despite all I have lived through since. The true identity of that child, his unique and veritable origin was that autumn day, leisured and sunny, away from the hasty, greedy lives of men.

To attain to that supreme identity, he still needed the firm certainty of having a native country, a past, a land—yes, a kingdom, from whence his dreams could arise towards that luminous moment he was alive in and without any thought of line five on that page in his passport.

THE FOLLOWING DAY AN OBLIQUE ECHO OFFERED AN UNEX-
pected response to those questions of origins and belonging
that so concerned me.

When I arrived at the Devil's Corner I saw Sarven seated
there beneath his sundial—even though on that day, windy as
it was and lit up by occasional flashes of sunlight, the hours
were no longer being recorded on the heavy dial, now in deep
shade. A man was sitting there opposite him and seemed
to be haranguing the old man furiously in Armenian. This
stranger was making fiery declarations with glaring eyes,
waving his hands about with fingers that seemed at times to
be bent back convulsively. Sarven was listening to him, rub-
bing his brow and uttering a grunt from time to time, but I
was unable to understand whether these indicated approval
or disagreement.

"What are they talking about?" I asked Vardan, who always enjoyed acting as interpreter, and he gave this summary:

"This fellow has come here in support of the 'fighters for national liberation,' which is what he calls the Armenians who are on trial. He wants to start a revolution now, an armed struggle, a 'war of independence to the last drop of blood' . . ."

"And what does Sarven say?"

"Hold on . . . Right, he's quoting a proverb. Oh, I've never heard that one before. 'He who speaks much, learns little' . . ."

"And what does the other one say?"

"He's still holding forth, without listening . . ."

At that moment the bench creaked heavily—we guessed that the old man was standing up and Vardan translated for me the concluding words he addressed to the young orator.

"This is what Sarven said: 'Now listen, my good fellow, if you look at the map of Armenia you'll see the Turks on one side and the Azeris on the other. And to the south, the Iranians. And even with your fine plans for liberty and independence, that's something you won't change. Not unless you can send the Armenians to the moon . . . So before they embark on a long and murderous war, your comrades ought to spend a little time studying geography . . .' In fact, I don't think Sarven really trusts him."

When the Soviet Empire collapsed, causing not just one war to break out but dozens, all across the country, I would remember that discussion. Millions dead, millions were exiled. What came back to me then was the image of those gatherings that used to come together around Sarven, such a variety of people. Not a nostalgic memory of a lost paradise and universal love (fond fantasies!) but the conviction that all that bloody internal strife could have been avoided. Perhaps all that was needed was for people to gather together on a day in September beneath a sundial, whose slow-moving hours would have called to a halt the frenzy, always false and excessively verbose, of what is claimed to be "great" History.

But, above all, what we had learned on that day from the conversation between the two men was that the judgment was imminent. The following day the "kingdom of Armenia" would learn the tribunal's verdict and the sentence, so long awaited and so dreaded, which would settle the fate of the loved ones of Sarven, Shamiram, and Gulizar.

VI

YET AT FIRST ON THAT DECISIVE DAY NOTHING NEW AND SPE-cial occurred. Apart, perhaps, from the first snow, which had arrived during the night with beautiful flakes that fluttered sleepily down through the dull air.

As I walked back from school with Vardan, he did not seem particularly anxious. In the room where he lived, there was no sign of any kind of danger threatening the tranquil-ity of the little Armenian community. No trace indicating a departure in preparation.

The only worrying feature was the absence of Shamiram and Gulizar, but no doubt they were at that moment pres-ent at the court hearing. The period of preventive detention had lasted for so long that, after several weeks, the ending of it was awaited as a relief, a deliverance from an interminable torment.

It was the visit of a neighbor which suddenly sped up the passage of time on that autumn afternoon. She did not come to the front door but knocked on the window, clearly trying to conceal her relationship with the Armenian tenants. Without offering any explanation, she handed Vardan a piece of paper, folded in half, upon which, when I glanced at it curiously, I recognized the same Armenian script as that of the newspapers that lay on Shamiram's table.

Vardan read through it. Then, as if the message had struck him as too improbable, he reread it, reciting the contents in a whisper. The look he then gave me seemed unaware that I was on tenterhooks. For several seconds he remained in a daze, then he donned his jacket again, put on the heavy boots he wore when we were doing our digging, and without really addressing his remarks to me, declared: "I've got to go there! It might still be possible to help them . . ."

I followed him, willy-nilly, bombarding him with questions to which he very likely had no answers.

"So, what's happening, Vardan? Have they been judged or not? What are you going to do now? Is Gulizar at the court, is that it? Tell me if I should go there on my own. No one would notice me . . ."

Not listening to me and in the grip of his idea, he opened the door and began walking along beside the old railway track that was already half buried in the snow. As we passed the last of the houses in the Devil's Corner, we saw Shamiram returning from the court, her head covered by a big black shawl.

As she reached us, she stopped for a moment and said a few words in Armenian, in tones that sounded to me more or less neutral, then she switched into Russian, so as not to exclude me from their conversation.

"You can go home quietly now. I don't think there's anything more to be done. Gulizar will soon be coming back too..."

She moved on, leaving us to choose between retracing our footsteps or continuing to walk—without any further purpose, as we now knew.

"So, what did he get, Gulizar's husband? Did Shamiram tell you or not?"

I spoke using a somewhat familiar and casual tone, so as to mitigate the shock of the sentence.

Vardan slowly carried on walking, with a dazed look, hesitating at every step. The words he spoke belonged to someone else, someone much older, someone defeated by life.

"Fifteen years. Less for the others. Between eight and twelve."

The most astonishing thing, if I think about it now, is that, at the time, this cruelly heavy punishment did not completely appall me. Subconsciously I must have added those fifteen years to my own age (thirteen plus fifteen) and the sum total of twenty-eight did not strike me as alarming, rather full of the promise that my future life as an adult would offer me. Yes, a young man, still under thirty, and who can now enjoy complete freedom. The notion of picturing in advance what destiny might await a woman, Gulizar, at the end of fifteen years, by which time she would be long past the age of forty, no, that idea did not occur to me. Still less, any image of a man, Gulizar's husband, as a prisoner who had served his sentence

ANDREÏ MAKINE

and would emerge, worn out and broken, at the age of almost
fifty, from that camp in the depths of the taiga.

My relatively casual attitude could also be explained by
the frequency with which, in those days, very long penal sentences were meted out by justice with few qualms. And we
knew, too, that in Stalin's time being sentenced to twenty
years of forced labor would be regarded as a harsh punishment, though a fairly common one.

"So, what are we going to do now?" I asked Vardan, still
adopting a light tone. "Shall we go back and listen to what else
Shamiram has to say?"

He stopped, irresolute, then, all at once, as if begging a
favor of me, said softly: "You know . . . I'd like to go up to our
hideaway . . . It may be the last time."

His humble tone of voice distressed me—he did not need
my permission, I thought. Then I realized that, after a week
of poor health, he was now quite frail and was not confident
of being able to climb up onto the rampart without my help.

So we walked towards the earthwork and embarked on a
climb, made difficult not only by Vardan's limping gait, as he
clung to my shoulder, but especially by the snow, the masses
of which had begun to soak the pathways leading up the slope.

When we reached the top, at the place where the cube was
situated, with its cosmonaut now covered in layers of ice, we
were so out of breath that we were not on the alert for anything unusual. I was about to start telling Vardan how I had
discovered the remains of the monks at the bottom of our pit,
when he suddenly cocked an ear, grew tense and, putting his
finger to his lips, signaled me to keep quiet.

With a little nod of his head he indicated the snow-covered ground around the cube and once more urged me to remain silent. I looked down and could scarcely suppress a whistle of amazement.

Muddy traces, clearly visible against the white, formed a trail of footprints along the side where the unfastened panel hid the entrance to our hideaway . . .

In a combative reaction against a possible intruder, I was on the point of rushing towards this entrance but was held back in time by Vardan. With an emphatic wink, he suggested I should do what he was about to do and, going first, with the cautiousness of a lookout, he pressed his brow against one of the plywood panels. I understood his intention and at almost the same moment we both of us peered through two adjacent slits into the interior of the cube.

What I saw was both very simple and utterly beyond words. In one of the corners of our refuge there was a woman leaning back against the inner wall. Her eyes were closed and her face was upturned towards the swirl of falling snow. A tall man, clad in a light summer shirt and gray trousers, held her by the waist and was gazing fixedly at her face, as if spellbound. The woman's coat was open, revealing a body that appeared to be naked. And the embrace he held her in made it look as if he sought to shield this nakedness against other eyes, against the cold . . . Or even to raise it up aloft, up into the white sky, in a flight through the whirling eddies of snowflakes.

This sight went far beyond all that I knew of life, of beauty, of love. And just at the edge of my vision, down below the aperture I was looking through, there was that mound of earth and bones, now being covered, little by little, by a carpet of snow.

The man suddenly came to life and looked round. We thought we must have betrayed our presence by the sound of ice crunching beneath our feet. Stepping back from the plywood wall, we moved away, and, with the haste of thieves on the run, began scrambling down the slope, no longer recognizing familiar landmarks, getting caught up in the rusty barbed wire and slipping on the grass which was thick with hoarfrost . . .

And it was in the midst of our flight that a frenzy of barking and whistles, coming from all sides, thrust us back into reality: it was the start of a man hunt. Our hideaway was being surrounded by a squad setting out in pursuit of an escaped prisoner.

Before their encirclement had tightened around the rampart, we succeeded in making our way through into the alleyways of the Corner. Out of breath and stumbling at every step, Vardan summoned up the strength to call out to me in a brief cry: "Whatever happens, not a word to anyone. Not a word!"

It upset me deeply that he should have believed me capable of wrongdoing, willing to denounce the couple we had come upon in our hideaway. It was only much later that the sense of his remark would become clear to me: Vardan was begging me not to add a single word to what we had seen, not to mar the unreal beauty of that embrace with a comment that would have destroyed the mystery of it. We must keep to ourselves that unspeakable moment of two lovers united beneath a slow fall of snow.

The truth of this would come home to me as, recalling those few seconds of contemplation, I realized that when I caught sight of the woman, her face and her eyes closed, I had not even recognized Gulizar!

No, nothing must be said at this moment, nothing put into words.

WHEN WE GOT BACK TO THE "KINGDOM," WE CAME UPON Shamiram in her room with the muslin curtains in the act of taking down from the wall the two photographs of the Armenian families. An open suitcase was already half filled with clothes and books.

"It's time for you to take your medicine, you know, Vardan," she said with a mildly reproachful air, as if, as children out at play, we had merely come back late for tea.

Vardan took off his muddy clothes and removed his heavy boots and it was then that his body could be seen in all its painful weakness. He was shivering violently and, as he drank the infusion Shamiram handed him, the light chattering of his teeth against the cup could be heard. He put on a pair of pajamas and got into bed. The coloring of his face kept changing, now pale, now ruddy, something I was used to noticing on his cheeks and forehead. His breathing was irregular as he tried to smile at me.

The noise of barking that we had heard, as we climbed down from the rampart, was rapidly getting nearer, and the sound of brutal shouting rang out through the district.

Shamiram came up to me and did something she had never done before, put her arms round me and embraced me with a tenderness that paralyzed me with emotion.

"I think you ought to leave now," she said gently. "Go home. You'll be safer there."

Her way of speaking to me, as to an adult, took me by surprise, as it always did, and, without even saying goodbye to them, I started for the door. I turned and saw that Vardan was concealing his stiletto beneath the covers on his bed. He waved vaguely to me, as to someone you expect to see again in another quarter of an hour or so.

Outside in the street several men in uniform were going from house to house knocking at doors and yelling at anyone walking along beside the old railway line. Beyond the disused warehouse buildings several dogs could be heard, ferociously barking themselves hoarse . . . Suddenly, coming from the rampart, the sound of a shot rang out, followed by two or three more and by their echoes reverberating in the alleyways of the Devil's Corner.

Deciding to wait for all this agitation to die down, I slipped into a space between two houses where the walls were almost touching. From there I could see the *izba* where Sarven had his lodgings, and his bench, covered in snow. The old Armenian emerged from the house a few seconds before a group of three armed men came to his door.

They demanded to see his papers, but he did not bat an eyelid and, in a manner both good-natured and sure of himself, he tapped his chest, and remarked calmly: "This is my passport, young men."

He had just come home after the court hearing and all his war decorations were pinned to his chest. I could see one of them was the Order of the Red Flag and there were several silver medals, those "For gallantry," the most prized among soldiers . . . This reply of his disconcerted the armed men. To save face, one of the NCOs lost his temper and began screeching, addressing Sarven with contempt and threatening to arrest him. At this, the old man, still with the calmness that comes from courage and indifference in the face of danger, turned round and unhooked his sundial from the wall of the house.

"It weighs a ton, this stone," he commented placidly. "We don't want it to come down on the head of a lad who's got a bit too excited . . ."

This observation brought the scene to a standstill: three irresolute armed men, stuck there in the muddy snow, confronted by a tall old man holding aloft the heavy stone face of a sundial and poised to defend himself.

From the other side of the road a call rang out—an officer approached, waving his arms and ordering his subordinates to come with him and search the labyrinth of the empty warehouses. The soldiers withdrew, Sarven put the slab down on the bench and went back into his house.

I thought this was the best moment for me to escape from the Corner.

An unfortunate miscalculation, for, when I reached the "Boulevard" which marked the boundary of the district, I saw that the road was barred by half a dozen soldiers who had dogs with them.

It was the sense of smell of those Alsatians that was my undoing. They picked up the scent of my shoes and exploded into a cacophony of barking, standing up on their hind legs and being held back on the leash with great difficulty. This reaction left their masters in no doubt. They thrust me aside and searched me on the spot. In the pockets of my fleece-lined jacket (the garment we all wore at the orphanage) they found the pair of pliers which I had used to extract the screws fastening the plywood in our hideaway and also those thick old nails, still smeared with mud, that I had picked up in the search for our "treasure."

Denial would have been pointless, all the more because, a few minutes later, on the path down from the rampart, the dogs discovered another of those ancient nails, which had fallen out of my pocket during our flight.

The speed at which my life now seemed to be turned upside down was rather like the interval between the moment when you feel a cup slipping from your grasp and the sound of it breaking. A brief zone between before and after, which, for me, only lasted an hour—the time between being searched and put into a van with little barred windows and our arrival at a police station, following which I was put into a prison cell for young offenders.

So there I was in the very same prison that we had so many times observed through holes pierced in the panels of our hideaway. Not in the main building where adults were locked up, including the Armenians under arrest, but in a long single-story annex which we could not see from the top of the rampart.

It was a cell measuring not much more than twelve feet by fifteen and some forty young prisoners had been crammed in. Dirty legs, heads, and bodies stuck out from every available space on the three tiers of beds. A world where cruelty reigned supreme, with contempt for the smallest weakness and a far more pitiless hatred than that which prevailed in the adult prison cells.

It was a sacred rule for new arrivals to be humiliated. The warder who led me in pointed me towards a berth that was doubtless the worst in the cell, on a very short bed, in a corner you could only get to by climbing up. But as soon as he had gone out and I was preparing to lie down there, several hands took hold of me and thrust me down onto the cement floor.

The "boss" of the cell did not intervene and let his henchmen have their way. After a moment of numbness, I fought back furiously, knowing from experience that showing any sign of weakness could only make matters worse for me. The ones who pounced on me reminded me of that gang Vardan had one day managed to deflect from the path of a couple of lovers. Yes, these were hardened young thugs and their only miscalculation was not knowing that I came from an orphanage where such fights to the death were a common sport.

I no longer had my armed belt, confiscated when they searched me, but I still had one of those thick, rusty nails which I had managed to conceal in my armpit. Several of my attackers were gashed by its point.

At the height of this ferocious hand to hand fighting, a bleak and woefully clear idea struck me: life was just continuing, harsh, stupid life, distancing me forever from what I had experienced in the "kingdom of Armenia" . . .

The uproar made by our brawling finally alerted the warder who came in and was probably salvation, for, as a result of the blows being landed on me, I was beginning to taste blood in my mouth. At the first sound of the key in the lock my assailants all rushed back onto their beds.

The man found me sitting there on the floor, with my mouth all bloody, one eyelid torn and not a single button left on my shirt. To avoid complicating the situation by seeking out the true culprits, he vented his spleen on me, the newcomer.

"Now listen to me, you wretch. If I hear any more of that racket, you'll go straight into solitary, with no bed and no food, understood?"

I did not protest, nor did I try to complain and point out my tormentors. This attitude won me a breathing space after the warder left. Or at least there was a strange moment of hesitation—even the "boss" did not know whether I should be punished more severely or left in peace for a while. I was now able to identify him, a stocky fellow with a bull-like neck and a grimace of disgust that never left his lips.

I got up, wiped the blood off my face with my shirt sleeve and went and stood in front of him.

"Now then, chief, would you like me to touch the sky?"

I put this question in a voice so free and fearless that even I was amazed.

His lips moved, and his blasé grimace, twisted in scorn, disappeared. Clearly disconcerted, he spat out: "Are you off your nut, or what? Touch the sky? . . . It's out there behind bars, the sky! And that's how it's going to stay."

I crouched down and, seeing that there were intrigued looks being directed at me from all the levels of beds, I spoke louder.

"Down here, just above the cement floor, it's the same air as out there, up with the clouds. It's the same sky and it starts here, close to the ground, under our feet . . ."

Objections and mockery rang out, but also sounds of agreement. And then a brief silence fell, as if they were each trying to work out what difference the fact of the sky having become so close made to their lives.

During the week that I was to spend in that cell Vardan's sky would save me from a surfeit of aggression and hence from many injuries and torments. My fellow prisoners must have believed I was suffering from a form of insanity, not really dangerous, almost amusing, yes, a type of fantastic folly that set me apart from what they considered to be their real life. Thus do madmen and poets sometimes escape from the trap of that communal existence, in which what rules the roost is our customs, our fears, our inability to love.

AFTER A WEEK THEY TOOK ME TO A LITTLE SMOKE-FILLED office where an examining magistrate interrogated me about my earth-moving activities, about that hole, which was six feet deep, after all, and, to make matters worse, located close to a "penitentiary establishment."

I quite quickly guessed that I was only a very small and fairly unimportant cog in an affair they were trying to unravel, or more precisely, to complicate, in order to launch a much more important inquiry.

The magistrate was clearly seeking to implicate as many as possible of the Armenians as being guilty—in his version of the events—of what he called "preparing to commit subversive acts." He found my replies disappointing.

"No, I dug the hole all by myself," I explained to him. After all, how could that friend of mine who was sick and kept having to stay in bed all the time, how could Vardan have helped me? No, I didn't know there were other Armenians in prison, and in any case, what was that to do with me? "I know some folks say they've been doing bad things, but the law's there to punish them, isn't it?"

The somewhat rustic candor I adopted in my answers must have seemed sufficiently convincing to him. But the one detail that risked undermining what I claimed in my story was the absence of any clear motive for my excavation work. Digging such a deep pit must surely have been occasioned by some specific goal. But I had no idea what purpose I could invent for it.

After more than an hour of questioning, the magistrate got up and called the guard to take me back to my cell. From being a witness, I was now becoming a suspect, if not an accomplice. And it was then that I caught sight of a ray of sunlight falling upon the face of the clock on the wall above the table and remembered Sarven.

"Comrade judge, alright. I'm going to confess!" I growled, still in naïve, somewhat rough tones. "That hole, I was looking for a treasure. You see, I'd dug up some silver coins there and I thought if I went down deeper, I might find a whole chest . . . They're in my bag, at the orphanage, those coins . . ."

He sent someone to find the bag . . . The coins Sarven had given me were there. I had smeared them with mud, as he had advised me. Together with a colleague, the judge examined them and, after sending me out of the room, they spent a moment discussing this "new factor in the inquiry." For a youth driven by a raging lust for material gain to be motivated by the desire to grow rich must have fitted in neatly with the logic of the world as they saw it.

The following morning I was released.

With the passing of the years I would come to realize that it was not actually my devious confession that changed the direction taken by the inquiry. No doubt the instruction not to "dig too deeply" into this business of the digging came from on high. For the very fact of our having dug that pit might be perceived as a sign of lax vigilance on the part of the forces of law and order, and, as one thing led to another, give credit to the idea of a vast conspiracy, including an escape plan by means of an underground tunnel—and all this under the very noses of the shamefully unobservant appropriate services.

More seriously still, revealing the reality of the tensions between ethnic groups within our country, where friendship between all the peoples of the planet was publicly proclaimed, would represent too great a risk ideologically. A few Armenians, who had been somewhat too disruptive, had been arrested, judged, sent to a camp, and the matter was closed. Why be too zealous? Any additional investigation could only give further dangerous publicity to this unfortunate case of separatist dissidence.

Be that as it may, I would later come to reflect, not without a smile, that it was that handful of coins, minted in the days of the last tsar, that had saved me from the ominous fate of "solitary, with no bed and no food" with which that screw had threatened me.

THE EXPERIENCE I GAINED DURING THAT PAINFUL WEEK DID not only relate to the extreme savagery that prevailed in the cell with the young offenders.

In my life I had already experienced, and would do so again, conditions of existence such as would reduce still further my willingness to believe in the basic goodness of human nature.

No, the real lesson I learned was a different one: the incredible speed at which the normal routine of life can erase the memory of events that seemed at the time to be of great importance, of people who, a few days earlier, constituted the most precious part of ourselves.

Back at the orphanage where, thanks to my spell in prison, I was awarded a spurious reputation as a hard man, there was now very little talk of the events that had so recently caused turmoil in that part of the town: the invasion by armed men,

the searches, the patrolling by Alsatian dogs . . . A fresh piece
of news was on everybody's minds: a new skating rink, the
first time artificial ice had been installed in the town, was
about to become the venue for an ice hockey match between
two flagship Siberian teams!

And furthermore, nobody seemed able to say anything very
precise about the events that had taken place at the Devil's
Corner. There were various versions which, when strung
together, added up to an already somewhat fictitious sequence
of events that did not quite tally. What they gave me was an
outsider's view of the drama in which I myself had to some
extent played a part.

Thus, there was talk of a failed escape; of a treasure buried by the Armenians after digging in the ramparts; of a pair
of lovers whom the dogs had chased along paths in the snow
. . . But I avoided appearing too inquisitive, for fear of giving
myself away by my own questions, and ending up back in
front of the magistrate.

Towards the end of the autumn, choosing the hour of dusk, I
went back to the Devil's Corner and the alleyways of the former "kingdom of Armenia."

The snow had covered everything and you would need
to have strolled through the district on a clear day at the
end of summer to be able to picture those old railway
tracks, now beneath a blanket of snow, as well as that bench
where, profiting from the warmth of the long September
afternoons, Sarven used to converse with his guests. And
in particular his sundial that used to hang on the timber

wall, that was now coated with white beneath the squalls of snowflakes.

Through the window of the room where Shamiram and Vardan had lived, I thought I could make out the violet traces of the muslin draperies, no doubt left for the landlady as a parting gift.

In a backyard, behind the fence, I caught sight of a man splitting logs. I went over to him and recognized one of the former prisoners, that man whose nose was marked by a deep scar. Wary of having spotted a potential prowler, he was still holding his axe as he approached me. I greeted him, still remembering his name and patronymic. He gave me a somewhat unyielding stare, which then softened.

"Oh, it's you! What are you doing in these parts? He's gone away now, your mate. You know that . . ."

I was both hopeful and apprehensive about what might come next. But, having long since acquired the habit of caution during his hard years in prison, he said nothing more.

Making every effort to keep my feelings hidden, I asked him: "And . . . how about the others? I mean . . . er . . . Gulizar and her . . . fiancé . . . her husband . . ."

He could have rebuffed me, and I was expecting it, either fiercely or in the fatherly tones of a proverb: "The more you learn, the faster you'll grow old." But the coarse and battered features of his face suddenly took on a lost expression, a gleam of compassion of which his tortured mask had never seemed to me to be capable.

"Listen . . . What happened, happened the way it did . . . And maybe it was better for them like that . . . A beautiful girl like her, sent to a camp wouldn't have lasted long . . ."

He fell silent, shaking his head, reflecting on the inevitable violations that a lovely young woman would have suffered, if imprisoned.

"Be we can still see her, can't we, that Princess Gulizar? Down there at the end of the alley, where she used to go to visit her fellow in prison . . ."

He gestured towards where the road turned off, at the edge of the district, directing his gaze that way with such visionary force that, involuntarily, I turned my head too, searching for a silhouette clad in black beyond the eddies of falling snow.

The door of his house creaked and I caught sight of a woman with russet hair, wearing an old sheepskin waistcoat. She greeted me with a nod and began gathering up the split logs to take them indoors. I recognized her as the woman who had been sitting next to this former prisoner with the broken nose on the evening of Ronin's birthday . . . Once again she reminded me of a woman I was sure I had seen in passing, sometime previously, but whose image I could not summon up in my memory . . .

Moving to pick up the logs that lay around the block, she bent down and around her neck I glimpsed the pale gleam of a necklace of bluish glass. Yes, that necklace was somehow familiar! I had a momentary flash of memory, but it vanished at once—I was still too deeply affected by having pictured the ghosts of the Armenians, moving through their kingdom amid the swirling snow.

I learned nothing further, and, in any case, I knew that if I had had the courage to question them, they would not have proved more talkative. The granite silences of people who had lived through the era of Stalin were well known to me.

As I made my way back along the alley that led from the Devil's Corner, I could hear the repeated dry crack of the axe against the block and then sometimes moments when it stopped. The man must have paused in his task, standing there and allowing his gaze to stray through that veil of white that was now being drawn across the last traces of the "kingdom."

When I reached the base of the rampart, I could see that the barbed wire had been repaired and, up at the top, a fence with wire netting had been erected around our plywood cube. I still had my pliers in my jacket pocket and under the cover of dusk, I began climbing up, cutting through the strands of wire where I could not step over them.

Up at the summit the cosmonaut was still there on the propaganda panel, but the wire screen kept me a yard away from it and prevented me from pressing my eye against one of our viewing slits.

I was preparing to go back down again when, beside the gaps Vardan had fashioned long ago with the help of his stiletto, I suddenly caught sight of some openings we had never seen there during the days of our adventures—five or six perfectly round apertures, punctuating the panel at the height of my chest.

Bullet holes.

OUR TEACHER, RONIN, SEEMED EQUALLY RELUCTANT TO share with me anything he might know about the last days of the Armenian community. Only once, when he came across me after school, did he speak to me about that luminous, tragic interlude.

"The most important thing, you know, is not to forget them. That's all they would have asked of us, if they were still able to talk to us, the way they used to, in those days, on Sarven's bench . . ."

We were standing in the middle of the courtyard where the asphalt surface still bore traces, now almost erased, of circles and polygons. And, without referring to it, I knew that, like me, Ronin was recalling the maple leaves the wind had scattered across those chalk lines, thus, according to Vardan, showing a way out that led far beyond their strict geometrical limits.

That brief conversation with Ronin—with its tenuous echo of those visits I used to make to the Devil's Corner — nevertheless made a deep impression on me that lasted for many years. To the extent that, wanting to be certain my memories of those few happy weeks in September would not fade, I often made the effort to recall the two photographs that hung on the wall in Shamiram's room. What I found was reassuring: nothing was forgotten. I remembered those two families in detail, with sadness, but serenely. I could recall their solemn faces, the way the boy held the bridle of his wooden horse and the doll with its two hands joined together in the arms of the little girl sitting on her mother's knee. Among all the memories, now vanished, and days long forgotten that would come to make up my life, the survival of these strangers' faces would never cease to amaze me.

As for the inhabitants of the "kingdom"—Vardan, Sarven, Shamiram, Gulizar, I have on occasion found myself conversing with them in my thoughts with a feeling of closeness and mutual understanding such as I have rarely experienced, even with friends and loved ones.

VII

THE VIVIDNESS OF THESE RECOLLECTIONS OF MY OWN DID not stop me noticing how memories of the brief tale inscribed in our hearts by the arrival and disappearance of the "kingdom of Armenia" were fading away. On occasion, as can happen a long time after a shipwreck, a piece of flotsam from those autumn days would rise to the surface, already worn smooth by the indifference of those who had never known them.

During the months that followed, a more or less fantastic rumor circulated which nobody, by the way, sought to verify. The details of it were now becoming the stuff of legend and seemed less important to people than the opening of a big sports equipment shop on the town's main avenue.

So it was said—and I was to hear several versions of the story—that the Armenian fugitive had escaped via a long tunnel which led through the prison drainage system all the way to the rampart. I knew that all this was untrue,

163

but, on the other hand, I had no knowledge of how the escape had actually ended or of the details of the capture. So I was forced to rely on all these strands of gossip that snaked their way through the town as far as the corridors of our school. Some people asserted that the escaped prisoner had been shot, along with his "accomplice." Others more inclined to embellish the facts swore they had heard, via a leak from an investigating magistrate, that the pair of lovers had managed to get away and hide in the labyrinth of the old warehouses. They were later said to have been seen catching a train in the direction of Central Asia. No, it was the Irkutsk-Moscow express, because, thanks to a handy connection, they were able to change trains and head southwards to Armenia and seek refuge among the mountains of their homeland . . .

What people were after, I now knew, was an amorous intrigue, the sentimental trappings of an affair, with heart-warming thrills. Yes, an honest-to-God love story.

But these fantasies, good as they were for a bit of worldly gossip, were clearly lacking in interest, compared with the number of goals scored in the latest ice hockey match or the forecast of a snowstorm just at the time of the winter holidays . . .

It was at that stage in my life that I came to realize just how insolently pitiless the cheerful platitude of the saying "Life goes on!" could be. So I had to resign myself to a form of amnesia, and a carefree outlook, a healthy instinct for happiness, a guarantee of social conformity. Yes, I had to learn how to turn my attention to other things, to forget about that doll with its hands pressed together in an old photograph taken in Armenia in 1913.

The cheerful geniality with which life urged us to move on, to view the next episode of its soap opera, yes, this implacable mechanism of existence, had an unexpected consequence for me: I suddenly began to regard with skepticism the books they made us read at school.

Every story had a memorable ending: a death, a victory, a defeat, the return of a prodigal son, a reunion between two souls abandoned by love . . . A gunshot, a boat breaking free from its moorings, dying words, which fell into place like the curtain at the end of a play. And to all of these things the authors would then add a few words of wisdom, for the edification of the reader.

But no book, I now began to notice, wrote about the terrifying banality with which life resumes its course, its clumsy plodding progress, giving the lie to all those passionate *pas de deux* and wise words engraved in marble.

From this I began to think that if a novelist had set out to tell the story of the "kingdom of Armenia," he would have faithfully transcribed all those anecdotes that were being hawked about in the town. An escape, an underground tunnel, gunshots—and a spectacular ending, one that focused on this episode, just as if the whole progress of the universe had really come to a halt there and as if, two days later, human stupidity would not be causing thousands of pairs of eyes to be concentrated on an icy pitch where a dozen men were knocking a black puck about with their sticks.

No, the departure of that little community had caused no interruption to this circus on ice, nor to the vortex of daily petty-mindedness, nor to the clownish antics of politicians.

I sensed that the only mystery worth exploring lay in our own ability to withstand the tide of folly that sought to sweep us far away from a past in which we had lost touch with the true essence of ourselves.

In March, six months after the departure of the Armenians, I was told that a woman had come to the orphanage and wanted to see me. I went down to meet her and recognized the old lady who had rented out half of her house at the Devil's Corner to Shamiram and Gulizar. She had received a gift the week before, a big parcel containing crystallized fruits and nuts which came from Armenia. There was also a package addressed to me.

Hiding away from the others, I opened this little cardboard box. Breathless with excitement, with feelings of joy, but also with a swift premonition of sadness, I withdrew from it Vardan's stiletto!

A short letter, written by Shamiram, informed me that the boy had died on New Year's Eve and that on the day before his death he had asked for this little dagger, with its silver hilt, to be sent to me.

ANDREÏ MAKINE

The sorrow that overcame me was not very far from a
wish no longer to exist, no longer to see the indifferent, sullen,
or laughing faces I encountered at school, a wish for an end
to this life of mine—not through suicide, but through some
miraculous withdrawal from this world and a new presence
under another sky, that sky where one evening I had heard
the rustle of wings stirring the air in the wake of a flight of
migrating geese.

My sorrow was increased when it struck me that the
writers we studied at school would doubtless have used my
friend's death for the last page of a book, rounding it off with
some elegant, lachrymose *vibrato* passage.

All lies and hypocrisy! I knew that the memory of that broken young life would be swiftly erased as the whole human
masquerade continued.

A naively juvenile plan then arose in my mind: to run away,
catch the Irkutsk-Moscow express, change trains, travel down
to the south, see the snowy peak of Mount Ararat . . . To redis-
cover an echo of that lost "kingdom."

And I was more than surprised—quite overcome—by
a coincidence that went far beyond this wild dream of mine
when, at the start of the autumn term, we were told that our
mathematics teacher, Ronin, would no longer be giving lessons at our school.

For he was the one who had gone to Armenia!

In my bemusement I called to mind the birthday celebra-
tion that had taken place a year previously, almost to the
day. Songs played on an old record player, the reminiscences
of war veterans, and, after the dinner, that moment when

Shamiram and Ronin said goodbye to one another, in a brief, timid embrace.

My joy was so extreme that, in an unspoken prayer, I longed for the passage of time to stop there, as it might in a book, upon this promise of happiness, upon this encounter between two beings, cruelly tested by life, infinitely far apart and suddenly united. I was ready to forgive everything in a novelist who might have ended the story with a scene that I dreamed about for a long time: carrying the very suitcase he had brought back with him on his return from the front, the one-armed Ronin steps down from the train and, amid the crowd gathered there on the station platform, he catches sight of Shamiram adjusting about her shoulders a great black shawl threaded through with silver.

VIII

THREE YEARS AGO I RETURNED TO THE TOWN WHERE I HAD spent my youth, and where, for a short while, the boy had lived, who, as I used to say, "taught me how to be someone I was not."

Everything about that brief episode of the "kingdom of Armenia," which had once seemed to me mysterious or obscured by censorship, had become surprisingly easy to unravel. A former school fellow of mine who now managed a local daily newspaper talked to me about the escape of Gulizar's husband, but he was already speaking of it as of an ancient legend. So I was at last able to reconstruct the sequence of events.

. . . The tunnel Vardan one day decides to dig, the explanation he gives to Gulizar, who tries to dissuade him from it, pointing out the futility of this childish plan. And then the successful escape: While the prisoner is being led back from the court, there is a moment of inattention on the part of the guards. Then follows his flight up onto the rampart towards our hideaway, where his beloved meets him . . . That propaganda cube becomes the only place in the world capable of offering them the respite of one last meeting.

Thus, from the start, it is an attempt destined to fail. All it offers is the hope of one last kiss before that gulf of fifteen years of separation . . .

My informant also suggested that the guards had probably been given orders to let the prisoner get away—so as to be able to follow him and arrest any possible accomplices.

"But the couple . . . you know, Gulizar and her man . . . Did they . . . survive or not?"

I put this question to him, amazed at how alive this past had remained within me. The sigh he gave resembled a yawn.

"To tell you the truth, I never heard anything more about it . . . For us, you know, that whole affair is as much ancient history as the Hundred Years' War."

Similarly late in the day came something else that gave all such information the dull aura of yesterday's news, I learned how much the "Armenian disease" had meanwhile become routinely curable. A doctor described to me the simple treatment which these days might have cured Vardan or, at the very least, enabled him to avoid those recurrent crises. Yes, what was then a fatal illness had since evolved into being an almost benign disorder.

The district known as the Devil's Corner no longer existed. The old wooden houses had been replaced by bijou "cottages" and the former warehouses had been rehabilitated and divided up into workspaces for artists and "creatives," including a gallery for contemporary art. In front of this building stood a vast sculpture, an agglomeration of machine parts, probably salvaged from one of the warehouses, which bore the title "Dynamism at rest."

The old railway lines had been removed and replaced by a cycle track which continued along the road beside the rampart. From being the "Boulevard of the Builders of Communism," this had been renamed a "Health Promenade." The lower part of the earth fortification had been excavated to house a car park. Along the ridge at the top, replacing the female *kolkhozniks*, workers, scientists, and cosmonauts of yesteryear, there were electronic screens, placed at an angle, which slid up and down with the regularity of automata, advertising now a four-by-four, now a Red Sea cruise.

Behind the rampart, the old monastery, formerly converted into a prison, had once again become . . . a monastery! The church, rebuilt, thrust its onion domes upwards, the gilding on them was too startlingly bright, like that of the icons within it: there had not yet been enough time for them to become tarnished by the smoke from candles.

On the site of our orphanage there stood a vast shopping mall and as I strolled along the arcades, I reflected that, in the prehistoric era of our Spartan childhood, the abundance of the goods now on display in this place would have overwhelmed us, like a science fiction dream or, more politically, like the worst caricature of the consumerism of modern society. So much electronic equipment, so many clothes, so much food! I was staggered, above all, by the variety of types of mobile phone and, in another section, the plethora of food mixers. With this array of devices, you could have made contact with every human being on earth and blended all the foodstuffs in the world! A very smartly dressed couple was having an argument over which type of blender to choose. This young married couple was using precise technical terms, demonstrating a complete understanding of all the functions of the apparatus they lusted after. I found it amusing to listen to this incomprehensible language and especially to reflect, albeit with alarm, that a great part of their lives might be taken up with dilemmas of this kind and that all those recent revolutions, wars, and upheavals in Russia had culminated in little domestic scenes like this. I think it was the wife who won the argument . . .

Then I thought about Shamiram's old coffee pot, the subtle sheen from the arabesque designs engraved in the silver, the muted gleam of it, which for me was so evocative of the colors of the "kingdom of Armenia."

And this new world, increasingly invasive and "blended," from Siberia to New York, would have found no scrap of land to give shelter to that little cohort of exiles, with their memories, their hopes, and those two family photographs in the room where Vardan slept on a bed made up of suitcases. From the top of the rampart the advertising slogans enjoined the multitudes to endlessly consume, to satisfy a myriad of instant desires, to be constantly "relocating," to blend all cultures together in one brew, to celebrate all things exotic.

Walking around the sites of those vanished times, I fell to wondering what there was that was exotic about Vardan's life and mine in those years when the communist empire was coming to an end. A large Siberian town, a poverty-stricken district, outside which people rarely strayed and, behind that rampart—those windows crisscrossed with thick iron bars, the antechamber to the camps. Such an existence could not fail to seem hideously cramped to the human beings of today, proud to be "citizens of the world" and swearing only by "world culture."

Yet this modernity, which claimed to be united by a connection to everything and everyone, was in reality closing in on itself with increasing deafness. Above all, as regards what Vardan had one day shown me through the slits in our plywood cube: That hand behind the iron bars—a prisoner who was trying to open a little narrow window in his cell. For a moment we had formed a bond with him that the most sophisticated "connectivity" will never attain. As we listened to the rustling sounds of a flight of migrating geese overhead, we thought of this man; perhaps he, too, felt at one with the freedom of their great beating wings, colored mauve by the setting sun.

Compared with Sarven's sundial, the new exoticisms seemed to me ludicrous, the time it told was eloquent of our own vulnerability in the face of history and the precious rarity of those moments when, gathered together, we could challenge this grim destiny with our fraternal support for those who were "letting their souls thaw out," as the men who came to the old Armenian's table used to put it.

As for the incessant preaching of humanism, that religion in which man believes himself to be God, I remembered that Shamiram never professed any kind of philanthropic credo.

In a small town in the Caucasus, devastated by an ethnic conflict, she took into her arms a child born of a rape and made him her son. The child's father was an Azeri, and therefore an enemy! But Shamiram transformed death into new life and hatred into love.

She gave to Vardan what had been lacking to that child from his birth: a maternal presence, the dream of a native land—an Armenia rich with a past of which he would be proud and, above all, the chance to feel that he was no mere accident in the turbulent flow of time.

And if, when I thought about him, I still had feelings of guilt that were hard to define, this related to an awareness that would surely grow only stronger with the passage of time. Having died just before he was fifteen, Vardan had never had the chance to know that other love—the intoxication of a passion, the adoration that worships a face, the heady fever of bodies attracted to one another by desire. Everything I myself aspired to and that, like many another man, I was due to discover, lose, find again, undervalue, begin searching for again, once more let slip . . .

"All that he has missed, missed forever, now!" There was a time when I would say this to myself, resenting my own over-generous compassion.

I was bitterly aware that every year that passed was going to distance me a little further from Vardan. He would remain fixed in his adolescence, on the threshold of a life of amorous adventure, while I would be moving on through the various stages of passionate exploration. Encounters, addictions of varying intensity, new attachments sought after, magnified, forgotten . . .

I felt as if I were looking through the rear window of a car—at a frail little figure left by the roadside, one that would grow ever smaller before it totally disappeared.

IT TOOK ME UNTIL I HAD LIVED THROUGH A WHOLE LIFETIME to realize that, rather than drawing further away from him, I was getting closer to him. For Vardan knew that, thanks to his illness, he had little time left to him and that the recurrence of his crises, which were becoming worse, foretold that the end would be soon. The fact of so young a boy having to live under such a sentence appalled me with its relentless countdown of days. But, as I grew older I came to realize that I was now on equal terms with that boy and that, as I lived on, I was like him, like all of us, increasingly swiftly using up the derisory quantity of days that separates us from death.

Quite simply from his childhood onwards, Vardan had been aware of the brevity of this borrowed time he lived on, and the strangeness of his behavior could be explained by a calm acceptance of what was going to happen to him. Hence, on occasion, that air of a wise and detached old man which showed through in him and which frightened us. And also his ability to sense the hidden meanings within our lives, which our own haste to grow up and enjoy them prevented us from seeing.

Without being fully aware of it, he lived with the feeling of no longer having a single minute to waste by taking part in all those games of rivalry and desire, the whole farce of human life that so attracted us. The few days that he had left to live must be used for what was essential. Yes, those maple leaves scattered across the polygons drawn on the asphalt; the sky that began beneath the soles of our shoes; the drunken prostitute whom he took it upon himself to assist, caring little that he might be seen, mocked, disapproved of.

Ronin had understood this strangeness of Vardan's when he spoke of "another principle of existence."

Thus, as life continued, I became closer again to that youth, whose life hovered on the brink of extinction. With constant bitterness, for which there was no remedy, I told myself that the only image of love that he would have known to marvel at would be forever limited to one seen through a slit cut in a plywood panel: that vision of an unmoving couple, united in a hypnotic embrace, indifferent to the rest of the world, beneath an indolent fall of snow . . . That unique image which, in reality, had lasted for a fleeting handful of seconds.

During the course of long years, I would hold onto the idea that the beauty of that intimate scene was but a humble gift of alms which Vardan's broken life granted him before it ended. A beautiful preliminary sketch, a luminous precursor, a discreet foretaste of the experience of physical love he could never enjoy.

But nowadays I am convinced that this moment of contemplation was nothing other than love itself, in its most earthly form, tragically brief and yet utterly complete.

No, there was nothing further to know, nothing more beautiful to long for. Just that woman with her eyes closed and the man gazing at the snowflakes as they settled upon the eyelids of the one he loved. Nothing more.

Those two lovers in their "kingdom of Armenia" that will live forever.

ANDREÏ MAKINE IS AN INTERNATIONALLY BESTSELLING author. He is the winner of the Goncourt Prize and the Médicis Prize, the two highest literary awards in France, for his novel *Dreams of My Russian Summers,* which was also a *New York Times* Notable Book and a *Los Angeles Times* Best Book of the Year. Makine was born in Siberia in 1957 and raised in the Soviet Union. Granted asylum in France in 1987, Makine was personally given French citizenship by President Jacques Chirac. He now lives in Paris. Arcade Publishing has published eleven of Makine's acclaimed novels in English.

GEOFFREY STRACHAN HAS TRANSLATED ALL OF ANDREÏ Makine's novels published in English to date. He was awarded the Scott Moncrieff Prize for his translation of *Dreams of My Russian Summers.* His translations also include novels by Jérôme Ferrari, Nathacha Appanah, and Yasmina Reza.